Judas Eye
and
Self-Portrait/Deathwatch

JUDAS EYE
and
SELF-PORTRAIT/DEATHWATCH

Breyten Breytenbach

faber and faber
LONDON · BOSTON

First published in 1988
by Faber and Faber Limited
3 Queen Square London WC1N 3AU

Printed in Great Britain by
Richard Clay Ltd, Bungay, Suffolk

British Library Cataloguing in Publication Data
Breytenbach, Breyten
Judas eye.
I. Title
828   PT6592.12.R4

ISBN 0–571–15122–1

Contents

JUDAS EYE

———

63 prison poems
of an indefinite colour
(1975–82)

FOR LADY ONE

1
The Undanced Dance

*an inside patched
with unlimited outside*

IED

HEART, WINTER, WOMBSICK, CAFARD,
MORTICE-WHEEL, FIRETALK, URD, TAKE
THIS GAP, DUGONG, GHONGGHONE, META
MORPHOUS, CONFITEOR, FREE AS BURD,
RIEN NE VA PLUS, METAMORPHEUS,
DANCE THE PIG, HOMO FACTRITUS,
ALARMBRA, SKEBENGA, PARADOGM,
METAMORPPHERISED, FALANCE, TONGUE
SERVICE, MOVES, (NEKRA), PIGHT
THE POKE, NEURILEMMA, PASSAGAGA
A VIDE, FATERLAND, MATRIX,
JAMMED, DOLL'S COUGHFIN, FROOT-ROT,
SEEDSOCK, BUNCHED, EJACTORATE,
GODFUSCATION, MICTURE, DHEU,
QUATSH! FREEDOOM,

memory one

I remember:
for that one measureless moment
my hands cupped around the sun
a cage
and I saw
fluttering, fleeter than any colour or outline
and I sipped
till my tongue was still with the pain:

destination

to the sea we cannot go back
the sea has grown old
with white wrinkles and foam around the lips

we cannot return to the desert
there's violence behind the dunes
ant-fortresses on their way to war
in pale valleys the jackals trot through light nights
each within the cool zareba of his shadowsteps

all the borders are now fronts and firelines
we are well up shit creek

here we shall dawdle
where the suburbs have been levelled
and soiled grave-diggers live in cellars
transparent as if of the present
self-contained like faucets
deaf to their own dripping
the blind things devouring corpses
with nothing to show
except cost-price second-mouth false teeth

here the hands of the sextons
are moving with wrinkles and the foam
from dark corpses they had to wash
perfuming bridegrooms for the bridal bed

here we tumble
implosively
to new interior boundaries

the dream

I dreamed:
I'm in a prison of white walls
where nobody knows me where voices
go absent in corridors where lights sough
my skull wheezes
I saw my self:
squat to shit in a bucket flies
come with the summer nights
the lights sigh white flames
I saw my name:
shifting down the lists with nobody
to read remember
ever more dimly through annual rings
curved into the white of the gaol

I awoke:
when the judas-eye looked a start at me

out there

'if words could speak words should have told...'
                    not so, Federico?
did you see it looming?
sparkspanking black horses in the night
with a jingling of stirrups
the way stars chink when you tread on them
to release a bruised odour,
was that the secret sign of fate
through the dark-hearted joy of the villages —
                    how did it go again?
                    — open wide the shutters
                    and put flowers
                    on balcony and windowsill
                    and sing for me
                    ah, the day smells of oranges —
divine this liberty and sweet is the sound!

or just beyond the orchard down by the river
where a rider might slice the moon
with his knife from its water
(and she no virgin),
did you know it then?
in Cordoba, no, Granada?
where gardens grow an Arabian calm
and each palmtree deep like deepsong
rising in the coiled night of the blood —
                    did you know
                    as you were taken to dig the grave
                    grey and grave the faint break of day
                    where you and your carcass would lie
                    with a bullet-hole between the buttocks —
                    why?

and you, Osip?
                    faulty like the very future,
you with the words a glass-clear bell in the nocturnal

bungle and botch of being human
                    making your lips to tremble
                    all down the thingamabody
                    to the fingers on the pad
                    where phalanxes are lips
                    beseeching a tongue
                    when paper is pale wasteland –
you who identified the predator lurking
behind the withered hand and the paranoid whiskers,
you who saw man indignifying man –
surely you must have recognized your destiny
snuffling for you,
the fool, the amnesiac
caricature with the shivers in a greatcoat,
wedged, lice-infested, in a cattle-truck
among the errant dead –
crazed one in the irrevocable extremes of some Siberia,
holy clown in a slave-camp –
                    till you were no more Osip, poet-person
                    but just a pile of rotted-bare
                    decay
                    spoor in the snow
                    twist in time
muttered muttering become wind in the wind –
why?

is yours the only course then, Hanshan?
shrieking monk on Cold Mountain
with your verses penned in brush and cloud
pearls of tears and frosted footfalls
going past Fate and Why
the way everything that lives must die
                    and live, and die,
and emerge from illusion's total truth,
and you never to have existed anyway?
that *so?*

is it thus,
        you shadows of conceit and phantoms of the well-
          versed heart?
unbolt those doors with their spider's work of locks
and push aside the bars of light —
behold, the night out there smells of oranges,
listen, there's windrhyme there are dreams there
        the voices of survivors

        I must go up to the ridges
        where aloes smoulder red bait for planets
        where ants build fortresses around a bride
        and a finger carelessly predicts the seasons in dust,
        I want to stroke the celestial dome
        must lie on earth
        to see mountains gambol,
        I wish to be a life
        as only death can still be pulsation ...

war

there is war: 'the land destroyed'
(so the Pondos have it);
when I clamber higher I spy through barred window
night's framed visage
(*and I a volunteer!*) —
then, below, I inflect my campaign,
whisper-bark my mandamuses,
over hill and dale of this tabletop
I dress and entrench my vocables: (the tin troops)
while canons wolf down the outermost skyline

the bifid route

I came to a cradle in the road
both feet still steady on the ground
to left and abaft: the ocean an unbridled song
but here where the path goes snaking higher
and hills spring up — as well as the etched slashes of rifts
and spinning plum-blue clouds on bulging blue branches —
here it was just about quiet;
                              had to laugh at the telephone wires though
long reeling takings of the breath
like your lines, Ez
                    I had to snigger
at the thought of communication

unreality can at times be a singeing flame
sucked from the heart to attempt the *move*
(away from the real?)
which is why I couldn't help but whinny
when thinking of you
dear Mister Mensch (forgive old 'un this unearthing
of your mortal frame to flesh it out with lifelike unreality
for this much must be clear:
                              I insist
on forcing you to backtalk in these stanzas)

(I) remember you in that cliché of my memory
your countenance a rictus satanicus grimace as if
they had you swallow a smileful of strychnine so
                    captivity poisons the blood
                         no?
                    agonizing wolf
    can taste it now
    this semen-spleen
                    (I) too am caged

14

'Tear Down Thy Vanity' you wrote
from your coop in the dust and the sun
on that small-town market square elsewhere
in some Italy
sure I'll try plucking out all cockiness
frustration too —
                    why I want to lid my eyes
to the white
walls
and wait for you to walk through steel and stone
like some ghost of the Prince's father —
why I don't wish to be in this writing —
bur 'tis easier for the camelword with no oil to its sound
to slither through the needle's mouth
than for the heart
to escape through that judas!

and open my eyes where freedom is
a verse after all filled with roominess
at a cleft in the road
                    on one hand the sea's own restless grammar
on the other the cool loophole of cloud and mount
and down the chiaroscuro gorges in the dappled light of orchards
my loved ones and my companions
                              and sweetheart she —
where once again I may cherish a choice
        is *this*
                at last way beyond the carry and care of hangman and
                    physician
                the wormwomb land of Poetry?

must annul my words antennule-like
    and have them slip through wire eyes
small lovers without vainglory of the Queen
soldiers, peasants, workers
who tunnelled your bones ripping silent
                        the garrulous thorax:
    for in the poem the snout gapes forever solitary

15

– perhaps burrowing the tongue in other orifices
                                        different projections of the blank
in other personae down distant meandering thought
– to recite the borrowing and spew same out –
but never will it be Another
talking images gush from the breast to be captured
                                        by hand from sourmouth
the hand is maw
                        an extension the heart's suck-n-pump . . .
I sorrowing here stand at one in the furnace of my verse

and a flame can never burn

where you? where outside?
I tried grasping the reason and the rhythm scanned
such a lot that the words became shallow graves
                                        depressions, collapsars
wee black holes burnt through the page
bullet-eyes to an evasive target

why bother (with) the word then?
shall I flog dulcet dainties like Sophocles or cheekily
                                        taunt like an Aristoph?
to fashion flesh
                like Rimbaud's alchemist
                from that which is imagined image? alone?
to take the word to pallet
and when you have raped the truth Oedipus
poke out the tentative eyes
in order to retain the metaphor?

do you write down this way to compensate
the absent inspiration – or is it vibration?
        or is the bottom line on poetry the out-squeezing of paradox
        the gap twixt so-saying and the unsayable
        to contain/describe with the likely that impossible
        twitching in the shadow of the mind
        mind you that is mind's shadow?

and poem piercing the paperthin prescribed frontier
pretends to the sublimation of unsolved irreconcilables
but butts on other bifurcations
                              and causes new discordancies
which bit by bit will rub the tongue raw
searching for (dis)solution as flame does for conflagration
and thus phonemes beteeth the dream
so too the word decays to sense the sentence to
                              diction direction to destination
and on the wheel will turn
to rot bringing decomposition which leads to rot

why bother with the word?

it is that plot of No Man's Parole
between where-all-description-fails
and death/described-failure/exhalation
(it is) specifically that tomb
which I must shore up with sound:
want to go down on a bed of words stop
have dream taste its own saliva stop
stallion for the nightmare stop

as I came to a crotch in the road
halfway along my life —
                              was I to cut the left-lying life in two?
both feet still solid on the soil
right and left the smoulder and flap of sea's
                              stuttering fire
smoke ingurgitating nightsky down a reddened gullet
and here higher under the ultimate freshness
                              of blue-quiffed trees
finally my people burgeoned: one old man armchaired
with eyes of sombre melancholia
one old woman laughing among magnolias to camouflage the weep
and with yet more things and configurations my siblings too
Bill and Jean brows meeting over chess a dislocated chimpanzee
headless on the bladed lawn and off to the side

lacertine-grey without a word to his name E.P. crouched to scratch
lizardly the one hand with the other

it was a concatenation of well-caressed faces:
nearly out of sight with premature stars about the head of his mount:
Federico — the boiled shirt and tie smudged with
                                        inky blood,
François bird-beaten on his gallows-tree, Osip
carrying his innards in the scoop of both hands,
also Pablo and Pablo — one a running sack of flames
the other a fogpond for frogs,
Dirk and Ingrid lost to the waist in conversation,
Hieronymous crying bats
and Edoardo so slender from pondering with the heart,
Basho's coniform hat against a wave-cleaving peak
just a palatine now in night's mouth . . .

Adonai elohenu a marine animal with cremated beak
croaked from the dissonant water
and *Adonai ehad* Saint John Cross groaned
hanging upspike down from yon tall crest
                                but Sensei guffawed in the dusk
and stuck a finger in the eye of the moon:
                        not one . . . not one . . .
and she my radiant Beatrice with the salient zygomatic bones
midnight-smooth limbs
brought me coals for the lips
beyond the cut in the earth after ocean's sob

'Two by two the flying birds return.
In these things there are a deeper meaning.'
(thus Tao Yuan-Ming consoled us then)

ah, Ez, I hereby close my saying more or less
from the forked stick to fashion a catapult:
now over to you:

december

following rhythm and road of a poem by Gary Snyder

Six a.m. – jingle
        of night commander
        speeding closer; keys crack
        down the corridor:
out there birds arbour tinkling
tiny bells: in the minute
meshed yard pansies fold open
like moths flagging down the day;
stretch the pallet with bedding on bunk;
in the section bath and shave.
        N— the cleaner, silent, pimpled
        white prison feet,
        brings the porridge, 'coffee', bread
        (who's trying to sell me short?)

Voice of section head: Jump to it!
Jump to it! Clean up! Move arse!
Inspection. Cement floor shimmering
a shaven face.

Out for exercise round
        and round the sightless pansies.
        Boer's cap-badge, whiskers, gleam.
        Cut the pocketchief
        lawn short
        and scour slop-bucket white:
        wind weeping in some
        wireless tree.

Ten-thirty lunch: boiled mealies,
beet, maybe meat. Dixies out!
Rinse off and wedge spoon in door.
Eleven o'clock the cell's locked:
                    midday snooze
        draw deep at the fag
        and listen to the Philistines rag.

Two o'clock. Taxi-pads across the floor
once more, Brasso on copper; Ghostkeeper's
      chill eye ringed by the judas;
      try making contact
      with connection.
      Cell ransacked — someone
      must have quacked.
      Stretch the pallet with bedding on bunk.

Three-thirty, graze — soup, 'coffee',
      yellow eye of butter
      framed by bread.
      Dixies out! Buck up!
Rinse off and spoon in door,
both shoes lined up
without feet on corridor floor.
      Four o'clock the cell is locked:
      Get up! Stand to!
      Gaol-bird countdown all motherfuckers you!

Lights on. Dusk
might be falling outside like prayer. Manna.
Listen how being locked up grinds.
                        Talk to self.

Condemns sing. Outside birds
mirror the tilted
tiny bell sounds; in the tight
meshed yard pansies fold together
like flags wording moths in the night.

Eight o'clock, slumbertime, lights out
      and fire of yearning.
Limelight and torch-blur on catwalk,
rifle-butts thud.
           Heart burns: sweet
           smoke in nostrils,
           thoughts scuffle:
A mugu sobs and bleats in the bush of sleep.

Zazen. Steel and concrete folds
where stars quiver;
        the guard's beat is god
        in the head —
        but stillness in the crop
        breath's penitential exercise.

Sit till midnight. Silently
        invoke this day's negative.
        Bow deep to the wall
        and stretch the pallet out on bunk.
        Stiff under sheets:
        white.

                Jingle
of night commander
speeding closer

the commitment

I suspect
but I won't put my life on the line
that there's a country
blue ribbon around a virgin's diffidence
behind the fast walls of this labyrinth

I dream
I can't say why
of a space as spacious as a dream
and light like tea-stains on the bridal gown

and hillocks not unlike freshly cudgelled brains
still smoking and quivering in the morning
of mountains with the colour of heavenly
blazes aged to ashes
the teeth of the dragon snow-bleached by sun
and that all this will inexplicably flare up in the night

that there's a disquieting sea
writing shorelines where whales will come calving
a white shakiness
and fertile zones for the mango and the pear
also the desert
for small mammals to gnibble at the wind
and at times a city like a blade oh so proud
with a rust-eaten grip in the withered hand

that the ribbon around the temples must rot away
and thoughts run free —
for this I don't give a poet's damn
for I am God
an impregnable keep

but something makes me wonder
I don't know what
about trains ripping a shimmering spear

and track in the vastness
and lorries and fleapits and pain
and cedar trees and confusion and landing strips
and vineyards and poverty
and sometimes the language rings a familiar bell
as if I could remember myself out of this predicament

then I dig down deeper into obscurity
and think
oh if only I could
what would happen
were I to climb up the walls
to chant from the parapet
'good morning Sout' Efrica I love thee!'

the wise fool and *ars poetica*

thus he decided to go forth
deeper into the region of vowels and consonants
where pure sounds sprout (though also other throatthrusts
and cleverlips cutting short the very breath:
mouse-birds among the Adam's figs), to areas
where sense and nonsense flourish where strophes
climb in odd places and strange and bitter fruit may happen –
or so he was told, and mused:
the oppressed goes out in the early morning
to look for solutions or failing all
an ersatz for the bloated fidgetiness; the fool
folds his hands and consumes his own flesh

it was quiet there (unpolluted by orb or orifice),
a thrumming silence, a calm redolent of smack
and suck, of oh and ay; he was at sea,
and deprived of the stick-and-track of needle and map
his eyes slithered over the boned black expanse
scouting for vegetation or visitation or just a flash
that might point the way to the well of inspiration,
even, if needs be (who was *he* to be bullfrogged
with pride?) a ladle of well-chewed cast-away victuals:
for a live dog is better than a dead lion

vanity, all vanity; all about him the barren whords
were as sand upon sand; he scanned his self
in the sand and moaned (thus it is written:
the offended will spit and shriek against the wind
but the lips of the fool will devour him
and darken the nest egg to nought):
'fathead, may you swallow an umbrella
and may it go open in your bowels...'
or: 'may you lose all your teeth except one
and that one be honing the ache...'
or: 'may the flies settle shuddering colonies
in the clefts of your armpits and the shuttle of your thighs...'

24

when at last there was a lunar paleness
and he as spent as time and tide, he went
to lay down arms and bones in the desert
(beyond horizons the neon verdict of night-clubs);
and tumbled into sleep: look, laid out he was
in a striped galabia with his lute as mute as the flower,
and a dog-tamed lion alive with the moon's silvery mane
came to sniff his breath and eavesdrop at his ear . . .

        so that now we'll never know
        whether the mangy meat-eater
        mustered sufficient curiosity or teeth
        to make an end
        to this poem

poem

'nicht auf meinem eigenen Mist gewachsen'

– willing, ready, receptive –
the solution is to be
self-evidently available,
you won't know when you're ripe
for divulgence, my friend

somewhere inside you
as in all of us
a man slumbers (or foots or stands),
the name is
Sleeping Beauty

the blind agriculturist
analphabetic sentinel
watching watch after watch
in the dew
never to decipher the nightbook
despite quiet glasseyes
brand-new anointed
won't wake up by hisself

the solution is to sleep wide agog
(death is only another
fuckform of life) in the walled garden
near the rosebush
under the moon grey matter
with her lobed light

a humble schnorrer
along the Highway
under night's table
(life is but another
ant-way of dying)
and not to be saddened
if you cannot grasp the antics
of the abacus

often it will be dry moths
with wings naked rustling
spiders with mirrors pinned to the back,
or diverse sounds
climbing up a ladder
to copulate
with white thoughts

your solution self-evidently
is to be at hand
for the worm, the poem
which, inheritor of your death
must perforce exploit your availability
right up to the focus

as the stork
without fuss
comes to nest
in the expectant woman's
other body

as St Januarius's
flaked blood
once a year in Naples
annotates a faked humidity

so that the poem again may
flow,
the worm like a languorous knife
through crust and crystals
of a precocious frost
bring corruption and relief

eating rain

it rains: does it notch tic-toc sounds?
oh heart of spades bloom pulsing the doom
'tis in dead hours when one walls in and sorts
out all breath that one knows: life is an ant-
line with neither nest nor baited goal
only a rumour of fumbling existence
shiverishly wiped from feeler on tentacle,
that they're but burnt black beats
all those nows and heres coagulated one
and one by one none, that one concocts
soldiering at beck and call of the pale prayed
queen's unseeing mystery: bleeding sweet
thus to play both blossom and stench
perpetuated on the tongue of the trembling ant-eater!

the visitation

19th April: today I saw the moon!

Milady,
just think that I could think
you were dead!
death is in the thinking – the thought
is death all ready

it just goes to show!

in a shadowy well within rising
walls open to the sky
one of my co-corpses suddenly yelled
and I looked
to not believe my eyes

a bird floats so high
that it is immobile and white
I thought
scared stiff by the scintillating tongue sun

and a Boer
one of the guardians of the Underworld
with his eyes screwed in the peak of his cap
claimed there goes your red-arsed locust

but ah Milady
it is you
half a pock-seared breast
a battered vision in a blue eye

eight months long you were dead
in my dreams
I learned how you were being dressed
for the gallows
wearing watertight latex bloomers
with the hem of your dress

29

stitched close around the knees
to intercept the female organs
the uterus the ovaries
plunging from you
when with a snap
you drop down the well
to break the day

I heard the hammer on the coffin's lid
knocking like the beating wings
of the broken-down owl
trapped by light

and at lunch the jester said
the grey shuddermush in my plastic bowl
must be the boiled brains of the moon

but you are alive
strung up high
hidden in the limpid day
and while I was thinking
you shone

the worst perhaps
is that without my knowing it
you still exist
even though I never see you
in my walls

Milady ah my lover *ma dame*
I salaam at your feet
and remember the ancient Arabs
already knew
a secret is in your blood —

and if you were to release it too often
you will bleed your death

prisoner

from here on you're the mugu who knows the moves,
skebenga, always out to score what you can —
often crazy for snout, lungs spongy with rotten issue
rolled in the Saturday of last month's *Cape Argus*
with stale news and mahala graft —
mouth grown green and old with the tongue's swarming curses —
nose institutionalized by stench of unfresh bodies,
sour spent breath of poophole pilots and other lallapipes —
your castrated mind, your cracks conceding promiscuity
and still no privacy to your solitude —
unending little humilities
and to stand for fuckall on your dig —
you are a well-adapted, numbered
file — dated, rehabilitated: learn
what's to be learned from boop education:
a prisoner must get to know his station

olives, forgotten motions of the hand, the word a craw softly
gnawing to crack the sealed spiralling ear's code, gold ring,
tenderness, crisp lettuce, sea song, sun's porch, running cheese,
newsprint wet with ink . . .

now and then like the shuddering of love making fire
in the harsh hour of dreams a memory shocks through you
                                        an absent reach
of wind in hair of rain on oakleaves
of a morning song in reeds your fingers touching hers
a sauntering crowd on the city streets
the sharp tang of car metal
caress of a new silk shirt's rustling colour
cigar smoke that twines out of deep dissolution
the blue saxophone pulsing exuberant
with wine's blended bouquet and flaming heart's blaze

31

from time to time everything
crumbles and the dullness of bone
again feels the flesh that was sweet —
in the white dead of night you see the laughter of her teeth —
soft slipping sweetness that was flesh

and under the scab you taste the pulsing tongue
like a beggar bum who knows all the moves,
skemuggel, always down and out to score what you can

time sequence

outside the deep sky was throughout a lilac blue
an ocean knowing no floor to its depth
but aware way below the surface
of forests and gorges with caverns
soft and sombre like water

and clouds   naked down sea-way
unaware of the reflections in many eyes
so that they moved in a dream
          clouds as huge-cool mountains
as yet without the scars of foot
or hoofprints with neither the eyebrows
nor the stains of birdflight
sheeted light   because they did not know
they were mountains

outside the reach of the labyrinth
desert curs crouched in the hills
with crimson tongues hanging
close to the porous earth
          the red walls of the prison
branded like sparks in their eyes
and sand piling up against the building
with the weight of soundlessness

salamanders carried the sun's light
of liquid glass
up the brick ramparts
          silence is a glass-green moth

within   in every cell was a breath
          those revoked to death
knotted new songs in strings
just as those sentenced to life
tried to recall old travel ditties
          keeper and bird kept an eye on one another
in this high house of Babylonian babbling

and played as if they'd never hear
    the bottomless earthtones of the tower beetle
    the firebrown instrument
slow   sad
flowing down some or other mirror passage

where often   between the quiver-wave and the ear's
tremble-tympan
the cello's varnished shudder hesitated
somewhere where Pablo Casals sat boring for painjoy
    irreproachable like sound —

transparenthesis

it is when an impersonal joy dawns on you
that something wheeling outside
and you a-twisting with it too
night transparent an indigo robe
relinquishes whitening colour in water's rush
a faded blue and then heavenly pallor
and of all the trinkets the morning-flame alone
will smoulder above the eastern rim —
rigid fire rigid fire right around the reach of the eye
and world a desert of miraculous wounds
a mountainscape's interiority unfolds
a flower passing away interminably

I shall take it that you then have to go down on the knees
absolutely outside the self
salaam and fingertiptouch the lips
tie tassles about the forehead and the wrists
recite yourself with ancient mouth-movements to some One
                                        or some Thing
pure gushing breaks forth from you
you bare and incorporate pulsation's intimate hidy-holes

— call it God cum liberation
    name that which comes tumbling from the mouth
    the surge of another's blood through your
    folds share the joy of that nothingness

the two scandaroons upsky flash the first
last orange sunswords —
thus to call upon the gods
outside time and time at the dead bird ritual of birth
to create everything out there inside for one henceforth:
it is good to comb the watch-arms over soft cyphers
as well while alive still to die

there is life

there are christs spiked against trees
prophets in the wilderness seized with fits
worshippers whose eyes bud under the sun
buddhas on one side conversing with figs

there is life greening in the clouds
while dolphins shred through loops of waves
the seagull's swerving gutlean shriek
and barefooted scragginess against mountainflanks

behind magnifying sky the crater's firespeech
inclines of snow like silences shifted
when heaven cracks open hairline wide
and out spill black legends the swallow the dove

there are bones that bind the earth
delight that breaks through what's time-bound
and blunderer droll notion though I may be
I'll still grow rich on daylight's beam

the scales flamed the whole night through
I might once have been a prisoner too
but here the heart's pulsing contract is spelled out:
we will all be naked a hundred years from now

mythmosaic

and when you get up
from having squatted behind the knees
there rests, no, rises
where shadows had eddied
fermenting smoke and freshly
prepared for flies
the pudding
(dessert, for purists)

thus the labyrinth bears
a bare pyramid

through prison runs the rumour that the world has come to naught
that catastrophe is upon us yes the bush war put fire to the dark
continent and backyards are littered with smouldering dead the milk
has been poisoned the mines the golden cloaci blown apart
a cloud of locusts has chittered through the chewing-gum factory
all plastic finally unsound Oyrope ravaged by internal contradictions
the heavens flucked into the sea all seaboards are awash
Franco and Stalin and Hitler and Nixon risen rule anew
all secret files in triplicate all negatives and positives and tapes
gone up in smoke
the Civil Service has chucked its regulations overboard
all gaol-keys have melted all sunlight gone grey
no more deep green stars no trees embroidered with birdsong
(and that we knew all along . . .)

> are we then
> do we have here
> miserable prisoners
> these hands of ours white
> as the hands
> of deceased albinos
> gnarled and vainly
> sheened with veins of porcelain
>   cups
> never drunk from
> do we hold here
> all that's left of life?

freezing-point

Legs wide he stands, the sun,
his chill dripping a flickering ice-cone,
a hairy flame at the core of coldness. A shivering sound
become stone. Legs wide he stands, back arched
against the livid circling heavens, and allows the mirror
to be seen: wherein no image glitters
nor anything but blank intensity.

Against the bathroom wall a sheet of steel
holds the liquid outlines of *bandiete* made to shave
without ever seeing clearly enough to slit their own throats:
the jugular pulses subterranean. In my chest I feel the apples
of decay and in my wrists the racing trains.
Now — after how many months of solitary confinement? —
a true mirror suddenly comes into my cell, a watching
pool of water, but below the frozen surface
a stool-pigeon beckons: a wrinkled blanched ape
most probably from China, gesticulating immoderately
and creasing my mouth into an inane grimace
when he catches my eye. Layer upon layer, grin on smirk
and the greyness of ash. His mouth is the bloody obscurity
of the apple's interior, livid fungus is flecked about his eyes.
A thing has come to grow in the brightness: and I am no longer alone.
I shall have to count my words.

How did this occur? The winter like apples
grey mouldering in the earth. And the wind
crumpling ash, rags, newspaperwords, cadavers of dogs,
bullet-cartridges, the open arteries of the roads:
the corpses, guts thick with blowflies in cupped hands.
And above the graphic of smoke swerve steel-eyed helicopters.
Higher still, a periscope rising out of the blue, the splinter of ice.

mirror-fresh reflection

you! you! you!
it's you mother-fucker I'm talking to
you ride with neither licence nor saddle
down the gutters and passages and compounds of my poems
my dying
you go subsoiling your lance deep through the blank domains
I so wanted to cultivate
for folk and fatherland
(but soon nothing will remain of the caboodle)
my dying
my handed-down perch of privileges
dumbly you come wooing my heart
the sorrow that I squirrelled away word for word
you're taking chances accursed one
go on take your chances

you with the yellow eyes and the left hand
you with the missing beard you with the sand
castelling your tongue
with your nine-year sentence like a pregnancy
I'll make of you chop-chop a widower
for you make me shiver
and moan
with pleasure
you lay the cold caresses of your lips
here on my life
chilblained here and here
come kiss me in my mouth
you hand-picked hound
come annul with lines my immature reflections
and weigh my slack wings down with stones

need I wait any longer
my pure white shadow Death?
ah, my very own intelligence spook
I'll be yours till the end of time
and you are
mine, mine, mine

the long arm

destitute I lifted mine eyes to the hills
and saw God semaphoring there, crowned on high
(and into the wind, so the message
went awry)

but the hooing and the haying didn't go on for long:
fire came mysteriously mushrooming from a bush
and immediately the Law caught hold of Him
for 'unauthorized trespassing on state property',
'negligence', 'squatting', 'crimen injuria'
and thrown in for good measure and a song
a few moreover suspected wrongs
perhaps against Culture or curia

now He's lying down this corridor in a cell
shaved mother naked with a stigma for a heart ...
a screw comes waggling his cap to tell
that matters look dinkum blind for the Old Bugger
cause apart from a suspended that's going to stand
(and a record as long as a testament from hell)
it appears there are still further charges to come
indeed, it is actually dawning on the land,
that 'security' was at stake as well

in the middle of the night

come rising in the middle of the night
the voices of those to be hanged within days
spliced already with the thin anguish
of taut ropes —
we each bear, looped over our thoughts
                                    like shadow
the noose, a cancer, splintering glass,
(yet: cruel the consciousness
that human lives must be emptied song by song —
or left brimful till the last?
like gulps from a glass)
                    what difference does it make
if you go down, a *bandiet* shot into space
or sporting silver socks, cigar in the kisser
on a fireline or in the ice-box-ocean
like a rasp among ancient reeds
or in the dark of some apartment hutch —
while alive we all bear the great divide
and shadow inside us
                        the knowledge

and breaks all at once (in the middle of the night)
through the white wall the memory of an image —
a rider on his horse momentarily immobilized
in the spattered silver jet
as he fords a river,
one gloved hand flung up in nonchalant salute,
standard Western cavalry outfit
(but a smile like a trout filleted under glass) —
        what matinée Buffalo Bill is this out of the blue
dangling from which chord of the mind
(before a TV set and fire with rain lacquering the tiles)
only to be hauled up now, why,
strangely branded and slabbed
on the retina of the imagination

while onto the roof drip
the dead blossoms?

   and so too this unforeseen shameless joy
that my thoughts can be with you despite all my fears,
that you share my intimacy
in the immense clustering and death of consciousness
                                        oh my wife

(while gulp by gulp shadowvoices are pitched out
in the middle of the night)

for the singers

for the singers
you singing from the dusky holes
as bees must do in a field with no flowers
you lamenting consolation where there's no relief
calling out to a Saviour for recourse and no rescue
can ever save you
singing as if your lives depend on it
and you know that your lives will hang

the singers, for you
who smell the obscurity
like cattle at the slaughtering places
the day is shrivelling night after night
hour by hour each voice is bent back
and threaded in the rope
the song a stupefaction?
can the voice go tell it on the mountain?
somewhere some ear is lying bodkin with the night

you will not see the veld with its odours
the smoke above the steel cities of our terrible land
not the birds thumb-tumbling from the clouds
or the tiny insects building huts in the loam
neither flash of motorcar or happiness of birth
or horse's gallop
or sun's fury and extravagance
nor the young women

only the rope will know you
and for now too the song
the heart, the heart a one-life-stand

but in the singing is the endlessness
of dying — with melancholy
praise the Lord Lord or the Prophet

who giveth peace when night lies
on its dark cutting edge
abidance from the Buddha behind joss-sticks
with his swollen apple-eyes of compassion –
what for? all over man
is death and dust
and only in others will he reverberate

could I do so I'd have made you
my guests where waves are beached
gravitated by the solidity
where people feast at silver linen tables
and why not the Scala and the Crazy Horse Saloon
the flatlands around Beograd
sea-bird islands close by Bergen
where there's dancing and hooting where winds
evoke chasms among the ridged peaks ...

what's tomorrow?
West? a paradise with lovely holiday chalets?
angels lay no eggs
a never-ending way with butterflies? the chilly
murmuring of pismire and worm
where everything becomes insignificant and is destroyed?
void in the cell?
the voices remain

everywhere man is dust and death and his moaning
                                    is as nothing
the one cleaves to the other and strings him up
the hands of the one claw open the other's gorge
so the law sings, such is man, thus the darkness rings
the outer and the inner
and life doesn't die
everywhere man lives on in the people

for you singing from the dark
for your ultimate daybreak – take, eat –
let your chant be like the breast
of the bird steeped in honey
and I shall retain the sweetness
for as long as my tongue can tremble
hanging in the mouth of bittersweet life

(19–9–75)

the conquerors

because we refused to see them as people
all that was inside us wasted away
and we find no more tears to bemoan our dying
       because we worked for nothing but hatred and fear
we ignored the human uprising clamouring for humane laws
and hoarsely tried to find ways out but all too late
the flowers in the fire

not a soul could care for our solutions

we are past all cluck-cluck comprehension
we are of some other dimension
we the children of Cain

       because we came before God with covetous pleading
God rendered our words cavernous and in vain
we now call out in chamber and garden upon porch
in the enclosures that we are the chosen folk

not a soul could be bothered about our hatred and our fear

the fruit petrifies on the tree the stalks
silt up on the land oil and salt grow scarce
the labourer's hand slips from the plough
to grasp for weapons
guns will not aid us   they will be lifted against us
for we are already out of time targets of dislocation
signs of annihilation   which will fade with time's consummation

       because we wished to pour lavishly of that blood
it grew heavy and weighed past the strength of our hands
these hands which into the sods we pitch
clouds big with voices

not a soul to weep over our talents and our death

what remains are coat, empty homestead, shaft of mine,
what cleaves till the root of being clots this sudden pain
of a dispossessed solitary path through the white bull's eye

the coming

they will come, many of them, so very many
that any count would be senseless, a tide
knows neither time nor number;
'like locusts!' the spokesmen cry:
but they will come as a tidal wave's backward surging,
like pilgrims on their way to the miracle spring
where the Virgin cleansed her feet,
like gypsies to a coronation,
like the scions of a wide-branching family
to the place where the roots run deep,
like Israelites of old to what must be possessed,
like winos to a watering-hole,
like migrant labourers,
like veterans to the whorled ingathering of a people,
like locusts, winged, against the ground, the nippers and the gnawers
they come, they will come
from all the outposts of promised and consolidated land
too miserable to bear maize or beast or any living thing
where death goes blown-bellied snuffling at the rubbish heaps

your enclosing perimeter will be penetrated,
your streets murmurous with scuffling feet,
your lah-dah neighbourhoods will hear the trumpeting of children's
    speech,
your apartment towers will teeter to the foundations
and you will be unable to make out time's hysteron proteron;
you will choke on the poult and splutter in protest
spraying your dress shirts with indignant whisky
since the old structures of self-evidence and safeguard and authority
will all of a sudden be pies in the sky;
you will resort to barking orders while burying
the family silver: how shallow the earth turns out to be!
you will seek entrenchment behind your churches' white-plastered
assurances, guidance in bankrupt dogmas, enlightenment in liberal
hand-acts of charity

your security forces, carapaced like tortoises,
will use baton bashings and tear-gas to try and subdue
the intractables to scarecrows and bugbears;
there will no doubt be bulletins and directives and decrees
and commissions of enquiry vigorously fumbling about in the dark
and pressure groups of uneasy citizens:
but the people will already have defied their fears
like tattered passbooks ripped up and rotting in the appointed places;
and your images on the TV altars will fade to fog in the void,
your ethereal voices croak ever more wispily

your cockatoos will be taken with seizures
and the hearts of your schipperkes will quake
for they will flex your fancy shrubs into frames for plastic shelters,
they will chant at the crossroads while raising up stocks,
their nags will lap the water from your swimming pools,
nappies will suck up the sun like flags of truce above your hedges,
and those lecherous enough will enter your choice acres
of *Grielum humifusum* and *Dorotheanthus bellidiformis*,
sighing, to publicly perpetrate life with supple black blades
and then with red mouths full of red tongues they will laugh

they come, they will come
and you will be stripped to the bone,
exposed at the road's end of too many transgressions,
your lives lying doggo behind smoked eyes for tens of fat years
will now see humanity face to face
– skeleton, wrinkle, flicker of compassion –
as in a glass, clearly

for Françooi Viljoen

there are things one never forgets oh dissemblers —
cat's paws of darkness over closed eyelids
the brief clear gaping of the bullet's cough
car headlamps slitting the night to ribbons
painted white masks of the buffoon and the whore
the hangman's laughter like a dose of strychnine
the flesh-coloured flame
                                that cannot scorch the satin purse
black rooks on red haystacks
a dwarf with a whistle on the elephant's back
the tower filled since years with whispering fire
the green swollen booming of the sea
the long broken downhill shuffle of old age
braking till it's worn to the knees —
these, the inalienable souvenirs
the heart's tiny mirrors lugged the length of the journey

we all walk that road
of life on its way to death —
murderers, burglars, drug addicts and firebugs
thugs, embezzlers, rapists
and fellow terrorists —
you like I tattooed in lineament and skin
single in our destiny —
till we climb through the gap
into the kitchen pantry
and the earth munches us to the bone
— 'finished; dispatched; cracked; home' —

go well friends by the light of the body
go well marked by what's never forgotten
to the final prison where all memory goes dark —
hamba kahle!

release

already glistening I arrive the first day
with angel choirs: yonder the feathered folk sing psalms
and my countenance smells sweet and my hands
embalmed – did I not with all my years put aside
the final ointment precisely for this encounter?
quietly I'll recline with bated joy
so as not to move earth this last leg

dance dust my beloved – why are your eyes now so dull?
let our friends gather the laurel runners
and weave them into wreaths of green victory;
no one should mourn lest the bier be upset,
for I am yours now slaked of all dishonour,
yours where dolphins wind-softly wheel in the palms,
yours all freaked free in the boweries of night

2
Time Out

---

the great task of the middle
is to not eke out
the edges entirely

memory two

he will remember —
broken dawn mornings, the city robed in grey
and the distant droning for no apparent reason —
tripple of hooves? a tump, a flood —
the relaxed warm spine in the bed,
steaming bowl of tea and palm-pale bread
and then, with rain flicking the frozen glass face
on a pushbike through the city's misty canyons
past trees all bloated and leaking and glittering
with fog, to the *dojo* (much later sun like a barking gardened dog),
the cool black folds of breath
imploding silence,
                            and soon, deep from the belly —
Maka Hanya Haramita Shingyo:

he will remember —
rough workers' garb of bottle brothers in the bistro,
salutations, clickety-clack of words rubbing import,
and knives, dark blush on white napkin of light
through a wineglass, red steak, salad green,
the gentle contact with comradely eyes
and up! to work!
smell of turpentine and fresh linen canvas

he will remember —
the glow of flames in eyes darkly dreamt
of the woman curled before the hearthed fire,
journeys paced in days through coils of mountains
so white that the eye feels skinned, and down
among rice paddies through gold-flecked Siena dusks,
he'll remember the woman looking for cockles
along the rim of the blue waters
edging a desert where a wind
huffs soundlessly, and is peeled black

57

he will remember —
the mad moon an embered hand
from the ocean making feathered papillae
of the silvered palm trees, and shadows
clotting as fancy takes them, coating,
carrying forests, croaking

he will remember —
the sun for one timeless beat
fluttering a blood-stained bird in his fingers
to soar like a wall way beyond
any sconce or dungeon's narrow reach:

gya tei gya tei hara-so gya tei
bô-ji so wa-ká

Hanya Shingyooo . . .

transit

this land is scored brown by winter
melancholy comes upon it with each evening's fall
when the sky cracks a ripe dove's egg
the veld notched and folded over with shadow
gnawed brown by the locust folk
singeing black tracks towards moisture or grass
and brown before that with primeval caresses
it's a nonchalant land

winter smoke folded over the earth
in the brown twilight nesting birds chitter
and bud on telephone wires
the sod pungent with winter smoke
made sweet by subterranean heat

in a convoy we journeyed southward
no one could hear the clacking of our shackles
the vehicles on the highway shiny-eyed owls
guzzling all travellers down tooth and flail
and only later spewing up the hair and the nails
we are indigestible! indivisible! free!
now wall-eyed at the peek of the pick-up van window
I see moon and stars swelling like tears
outside the sweep of time's orbit

this land is all the seasons of the night
now and then we rattled through dead country towns
where no one could hear the clocking of our shackles
through empty streets flared by lines of shop windows
with glass-bound mannequins coldly mumming the latest styles
                    and softly walk-softly a black petrol jockey
hooded in grey balaclava and greyer greatcoat
the enduring ghost watching all things come and go

in the small hours a frostfall of stars
perhaps there were jackals in the hills
but by the first shimmer of morning
the world was too cold for kapok
and when we had to fill up with fuel
it was on an island in a sea of visions
of naked bush and grey land sea-deserted
a million years ago
                              early labourers
were on the way from nowhere to work
trudging all behind their cold footsteps
under the live foam of the clouds
and could not hear the clicking of our shackles

deeper south the mountain-chains were
white mirrored heliographs peaking above the green ambush
and regimentation of vineyards in the lowlands
humble indentations of the landman's investiture
glassy slit veins of water waiting for the spring

again evening came bruising through
                              only one other phase of winter's invention
each journey has its time-bound reach and intention
just as the verse on the line must know the point of its turning
and above the new prison the smoky moon was burning
a pale ship intact on frozen black sand
in the east a crackling ice palace lay stranded

through the hatches sweet swollen odour of nightflowers
magnolia and sea mixing in bruised evening delight
the clickclackclocked throats of the toads
the inquisitive patter and twitter of peewits
and with growing light the seagull's grey commentary
upon the sfumato signature of this seaboard
lifting mists against the mountain's solid obscurity

like silver thoughts the clouds will roll open
how magnificent the earth below!

                                        10/11–8–77

at South Hill

It may well be that this south binds neither heaven nor earth
given the wall of silence, a malnutrition of thought
and poverty of feeling, because echoes walk talking
in circles with no point of departure.
The infinite is that which spins open within your limit-lines
when you hit upon silences in the rhymeless unreasonable pace,
history from which black-beetles flow —
a separate silence — other verbose spillways
of the lobe. Make of the day an earth.
It is blown away, and in the memory already rises
the damp smell of sods fresh as garden greens.
But especially the night brings phantom images:
limitless mutations of anxiety and pain:
crumbling houses: corpses of loved ones with nails like moons
waxing clodded over in wretched casks.
Then you look for containment, mistiness, the whisper
of silentsound in cataracts of ink.
And trust that the words may forget you.

I planted beans at the foot of South Hill;
grass came up and the shoots are few and far between.
I'm out of bed with the cock to thin out the weeds
and the field must be worked over.
Then I remember my eyes, rest my wrists, raise my head
to peer at South Hill
where birds on the wing wheel hither and yon in pairs.
With the night I carry home on my back
the moon and the rake.
The cowpath is narrow, the bushes here so dense and high
that dewdrops pearl through my outer garment.
In all these things a deep meaning lies hidden —
only, when I try to formulmouth it
I forget the words.

white lines

vectatio, interque, et mutata regos vigorem dant

the heaving green slopes of the mountain-chain
the roaring roofs
and up high the caps and peaks of white eternity
silent as an edge (a ridge, a ledge) of foam
all about heaven's hem
and under leafy crests are the tunnels and caves
of a darker expanse
sunbeams crackling like butterflies
nights the white-bled moon is impaled on twigs
then the rising throat-sick sounds of power-saws
the way blind foxes howl for the moon
and the quivering axes all silvery voiced
t-i-i-i-mmm-bb-e-e-errr!
birds their feathers heavy with dew
wheel flap-winged above the fog in the hollows
the entire mountain goes *tic-tic-tic*
logs come sledging down the incline
like heavy tongues
the pale slash in the earth
the river seething and whirling and boiling its froth
where it spews from the heights a rain of sounds
stones honed white
eel and trout
till it takes on the blunt trunks
bigmammycrocodiles
pencils from the kindergarten of giants
to the sawmills where odour which seeped
through sap into the trees
can again be released;
then boat, house, paper, word —
and somewhere a moon mounts
whitely from the verse

sanctuary

from the very start it was destined to be thus
that you would cast us to one side
first with jeers and gossip talk
blunt clasp-knives laying bludgeons bare
then with mockery and blatant blacking of names
as we moved further out from the circle
of joviality the supple lattice-work of shadows
below fig trees the dreams of mouse-birds
I with my grand-dad a brittle bone-bundle on the back
and my father a stumbling close at hand
away from ancient orchards the rippling tranquillity of ring-walls
tomato fields under sprinkled irrigation
silverish landscapes under speeding cloud —

there were insects in your beards
a slipperiness about the supple pips of your eyes
and weak spittle-threads twined red around the tongues
but your smothered laughter and jests were worse than dog-barks
you high priests of bigotry —

the further you chased us the more impudent you became
regressing mindlessly to brutal archetypal ways
rooting communally for a psychic amnesia
under mud lies buried the god idea of pigs —

when night shrank you drove us along other roads
I with my grand-dad huffing like heavy wings on my hump
and my father a mumbling closer at hand
till we ran for sanctuary in the deer park
and then in barbarous blood-lust you broke the zoo gates
                                    open too —

and under rents in the stillness
bleak the inlay the ribbing of uproar and rot
we who had been dissenters were now the hunted prey

blundering through hedges
across whisper-filled savannas trying to break free
                                        to a new day
among zebras whose lines had flowed away
and buffaloes with hides gnawed bright by the lice
old age is a parasite —

and on our trail you came snickering degenerate laughter
by the light of battle-axes and a sputtering of flares
your dim heads with bruise-marked facial features
mouths slackened into idiotic leers
and you no longer had the knowledge of who you were
nor laws linking freedom to accountability
nor conscience fielded by boundaries of reference —
but that we must be crushed one and all

judgement

'Mine eyes have seen the glory
of the coming of the Lord'

These eyes have seen the downfall of the whorld
in a concert hall
as the conductor mouthed his stretched howl to heaven
singing
till blood spouted through his waistcoat
pearl buttons spattering all about
and the orchestra with their fisted cheeks of putti and eyes
                                                    of nothingness
tried to find sanctuary for their tunekeeping breaths
in tubas, French horns, piccolos, trombones —
and the first violin fell upon the lean sound of his bow
his Stradivarius a platter bulging with entrails
and *cognoscenti* standing on their *fauteuils*
draped in fur and mink abruptly alive with moths
spiders blowflies sandflies hornets midges wasps mites
and the cupola a yawning pit
of sulphur, fiery slopes, the hanging gardens of the void,
    godvomit, angelflesh in hunks, Muhammad's donkey —
and as ants streamed from the floor under my shoe
a huge black roaring imploded
(one can go on falling this way
for ever)

At the station panic-stricken fugitives engulfed one another
a perpetual shrieking streaked the sky
light yellow in colour
the black signal of an exclamation mark above the locomotive
but I rammed a clear passage for my family
and when the coupé was scarlet with humankind —
my brother with his thin grey hairless skull
sitting there the last in line —
they forced me through the bursting window
westwards! westwards! westwards!
untergang des abendlandes

the train sobbed under a cascade of clouds
cleaving the land a hundred miles the hour
and clinging outside to the grinding coach
I saw the narrow-eyed tunnel approaching
and I saw the narrow-minded tunnel explode

As snow began to fall
it can go on falling this way
for ever
snow with seals and tassels and fluff
I saw on a dirt track alongside the ice-stalked rails
a pack of belled mongrels hunting some small animal down —
grey dogs, shimmering dogs, stinking dogs, blind
driven dog dogs
like bridal ribbons on the wind their streaming thoughtlike saliva
their insipid tongues hung from shadows of snow
and their prey covered in a thick chocolate pelt
bigger than a mole but not yet the size of a bear-cub
tried to burrow itself into the white sod at my feet —
and I rescued him — (which is to say)
green was the firmament and the dust aflame
the trees flocked with swans —
and far ahead a tunnel lured us on, or was it a trench
gullying under the transparent rails
back through to another world
of dove pasty and days of yore and wine? —
to that destination I wore the breathing pelt
while the dogs broke wind and tore the wraiths to pieces

And the portals were strewn with the teeth and the hands
of the philharmonic orchestra

on the hill

From a few of the hillocks pilgrim-trees stand forth
miraculous indelible bloodstains quicksanded
in their shifting shadows.
Below the botches the gravestones, swarming billboards:
many of his uncles and aunts were planted
in this conscription and nothing ever showed blade.
In the ersatz marble above each couple the epitaphs
are more often than not comic dialogues quoted
from one fictitious bible or another.

Homesteads are always built on the hill-tops;
tilted vines skirt and encircle the slopes
lacing the flanks of the vulval valleys.
Layer upon layer
small bird-shadows drape the vine leaves.

It is sobbingly hot. The neighbouring farmers on the nearby summit –
two brothers with matching pairs of braces – pot
shabby carrier pigeons from a high ledge
using automatics fitted with silencers.
Sht! Sht! and the birds with their sudden red letters
fall like clusters of grapes to the ground will fall
to bleed the love greetings.

Down on his knees he digs into the gritty surface.
Sweat runs like tears over the crotch of his nose. He unearths
what remains of a pair of jeans, a checked shirt: the clothes
the writer wore when he wanted to write.
A shadow strokes his hands and hastily
he tops up the grave: the woman stands there legs astride
balanced against the sun so that he can hear
her small hairy clock choking time.

But everywhere under the sand of the crest
are archaeological strata, layer upon layer

of grey relics. He digs a second hole and up comes a book
bound in red mouldy leather
and thick with ideograms.
Perhaps *this* was the collection of primordial ideas.
(Each hill turns out to be a fastness.)

feedback

this awareness-stalk reptile upright
pendulum-pedunculate-flowering in mirror-knowing
is what it's all about;
these corms and internodes on paper (carefully scanned)
there but to knot the mirror
drawing up being
in which you can just dip acquaintance
(or the other way round) (watch worms stalking the whitesong)
(language is after all the undoing of image)
enfin, if there were ever to be an asideable you
which between you and me is not to the point
seeing as how I keep nourishing you in my bosom
with liberty, that you may play with protuberance and sac
like a dinosaur frisking through the maze

whence? calyxed? blown from the primordial pot-hole
of course deep down where light and darkness couple
crying to high heaven (song of the Big Bang)
leaving language as festering injury
to the tree-knowledge of life and death
(and of death)
and *that* time-bound with the thrisk of dust
spelling rune and symbol and now computer codes –
how far back? how am I to count light and stammering
in umteens? or recount
where fingers start prying (into) obscurity
as glow-worms (let the maggots shed their vision)
shoed, fleamed, localized (where reflection is deflected
as swellings on the lateral cortical lobe)
in Broca's area (broken too) and dotted there
a bump known as Wernicke – wer? Nick?
jedenfalls nicht ick . . .
sprouted from my blindhood
I would wish for it to have been unique
but share it with pelican and yeti

the uptight präsident the babbler
and maybe (after all) the garden microbe

whereto mirror mirror of my hand?
oh imperfect matrix so endlessly perfected
irradiated with dismantling, core-sick under the bracts
or glass eyelids, self-stem-stunned
the better to explode infinitely in star-cum-
astral excacalation –
until hopefully (so to speak or fabulate)
the flower falls silent before the unthinkable –
how glorious! glorious! glorious! then to be
gobbled up by the light-declining Tongue!

lullaby

Schluf mine faygele
Mach tzu dine aygele
Eye lu lu lu

Close tight your eyes my love
Hush now my little dove

For the mouse in the kiss
For the blood in the shoe

Guernica Madrid Babi-Yar
Cyprus Belfast Suez
Athens Luanda Santiago
Santiago Hanoi My Lai Pnom-Penh
Hué Praha Budapest
Sabra Chatilla

Schluf geshmak mine kind
Schluf un zai-gezund
Eye lu lu lu

Ai
Sleep deep my wondrous child
Sleep stiff and still and blind

Ravensbrücken Belzec
Sobibor Bergen-Belsen
Majdanek Chelmno Treblinka
Auschwitz

The people are in the kraal
And with first light of morrow
Here's two socks bone-white as sorrow

And sleep piccaninny
And all the night-hooded names
I'm not yet allowed to say

What blackens the tongue
With the stone of its closeness
The tongue makes black

Aia lu du-du

the tree

Within the night the tree fully bottled
her blossoms darkened moons rocking on the twigs
fine as an eyelash across the moon
fine as the gnat's spine
her blossoms a thought-flow of fruit-sucking bats
each an ambush, a pulsebeat whirled into the hairy wrapping
            of its own pursed wings
her blossoms muffled throb of bells with powdered tongues
and the night entirely within the tree
till the train speeds past in steam and wind and a chatter of lights
knifing, marrowing over tiny moon-wet teeth of the suck-mice
with the shattered laughter of glass shards.

My wife: gazes at me by the dim come-hither glow
of rocking light bulbs and the landscape screams past
a hoarse throat
so black, so grey, so much like a crackle of darkness then
the white
handkerchiefs of a tree in bloom
taking its leave. I kiss her on the wet
whitishness of teeth between two wings dipped in silvery
blood about her mouth
and feel a shudder like a train streaking through me.

We are in the *rapide* on its steel blade to Marseilles
and M with us in the compartment:
M layabout companion of my youth
fresh from the grave, membrane yellow and loose as a dismembered
        skeleton in skin after eleven years in the prison cell
hard-up, harbourless, but now there's a song burbling
between the cigarette butts of his teeth.
In the red sand strewn over the coach floor
oval sculptures rest penis-smooth
to the soft flesh of the palms.

73

But when I hear the conductor come clickety-click
clicking down the corridor I lift out the heavy dressed
headstone and hide it away in the toilet
to notch under my fingertips the strange inscriptions
like notes of erosion in bone.

M has no ticket.
We roll him in a purple blanket
and stow him up on the baggage rack.
He is a king as dead as a rat.
He is a tree bled entirely white.
He is a knife in the guise of a bat.
He rocks
darkened moon ploughshare in the throat.

Chopin's fingers

to float to the surface from night's pond,
debris, putrid mirror, the noose of darkness
still narrowing the neck, the tune of nocturnal colours
which purified is now but water,
and to try hiding in the light — mouthing
the ballad of absence in a long-forgotten measure —
I wake up with the wet taste of ivory and of rook

knowledge of pain and consciousness of death —
the private careening, vacillation and demise of the impulse
within monotonous walls of the cell, minute red mimicough
                                          on the meagre grass —
but also the municipal
abdication: the light-exploding levelling
when systems fold, the communal inner space
a public hole without circumference

and knowing that this knowledge is blind, instinctive
stench from birth —
and the realization never realized that this pure vision
of blinding knowledge —
when with neither rhyme nor reason the shaft of knowing
nibbles around ancient edges of the well —
is an amulet, keening protection against death

thus alone do you dare to dance, aware of the laws
of captivity — never to trust, that betrayal will be
for a slice of bread, a vague promise of parole
or the small preferment to pimp — and to rely,
ensnared, on the loyalty of other cells, self-bent,
bodies stuffed with dying, other mutations of the self:
to save the grey moth under the shower

why is there singing in the slave quarters?
all dying is double, multiplied stains

in the shards — but imagination's plicae
fade away and the unthinkable finds its shape:
in a glass case I see you. I see us each
an individual wilting — sun moths — ah, to live
in this absurd world if only momentarily

with the earnestness of a flower —
to hold on to your image as a screening
from death's
deeper insight, my mask,
my mate,
my amulet,
my murmurous healing of the flame,
my minuscule moment of rook and ivory

father

and you came forth from the old patriarch's loins,
from a clan of hard and bitter inlanders:
drifters who trekked a dusty heaven in their quest
for the subterranean waterstar, for a course, for a pass,
for the satisfaction of threshing-floor and haystacks;
the interior a sea with grey crests, with brown crests,
the donkey-cart a caravel setting sail; die-hards
whose blood even the ants could not disperse,
rebels, nomads
through the wilderness they named life;
wheat one year and khaki-weed when the seasons turn;
from fatling and kitchen garden to goatherd and task-work,
from farmstead to squatter's shack; leggings and *velskoene*,
turtle-doves and locusts, jackals and shadowcurs;
    iguanas he strung up in the kloofs at full moon;
he had no book-learning, but decency to spare and share
and his heart was a bible;
in his sombre eyes he could hold the mountains
        to look for the hidy-holes of the morning star,
his hands giant shells filled with the reverberations of the earth:

and he died and was gathered in among his fathers,
he died and climbed into the ground
to sit mumbling among the quartz chips and clods of clay
where bushy-haired roots fiercely track the water down
        and rock crystallizes colour layer upon layer,
he died with the first dew and clambered into the trees,
the sun a light mantle on his shoulders,
his hair alive with cawing crows:

'love one another', his teeth signal in the wind,
the flesh passes, peeling away blue,
the shells grow luminous: (at times, I know, I am the pod
in which his restless bones knock and rod):

and you,
have you truly harnessed that restless blood?
I remember you out on the veranda your dark eyes
fixing the small foxes in the vineyards
and the shadows rushing from the hills,
your hands salty and damp, your boots
staking out their claim, limber and brown
you scatter rubies across the grass, crackle of glass;
I see you walking tall under the fruit trees
conversing with twilight configurations, how few your words;
after supper you lay out your evening prayers like peasant bread on a
    linen table-cloth;
you sit forked upon your steed to scout over the horizon,
                        over the obstacles in the offing;
you hunker on the mountain top with your ruminations
                        down below in the sweet valleys
and you summon the feathered ones, fiskal shrike, sparrow,
                        wagtail and swallow;
you wait on the high dune caressing with knitted brows the greenwater,
the white horses, the godsend:

and now you are old and just a breath short of eternity,
you will live on for ever
in this clan of hard and bitter inlanders,
travellers hunched round campfires in the nocturnal skies,
the great place of outspanning,
till first light rises from the earth and the erring is resumed:
now you are old and darkened: and I have your bones
                        your deep blood
and the soughing of your breast:
oh father, bless me before you go

you come only to say thanks for the Christmas card, Pa —
but good father, there's so much more I wish you to ask:
for my shoulder to lean on
that I may feel your hands this last stretch of the road
like long ago when you took me riding pickabback,
for me to tell you we're but a single dream of the stream
lighting up the eyes till they break inward (you know
better: the gobbler, his trump,
the wrecker's wearisome tooth
gnawing deep at the whorls of life,
wanting to laugh out white,
know of shadows flecking the plot
where the birth-hole is opening wide)

why this serene sorrow, Oubaas?
don't go! ask me to lie this one last time
to you (and me): to chase away with stammering words
those wings come to shake a farewell in your eyes,
the black wind draping this peninsula with flags
dulling throb by sob the big mountain drum beat
till a thick green sea spills its flood across the dunes

because there's so much I still want to ask
and confess over your veins and callouses —
blind as a child I'd like to be your staff

stay another season, root of my being,
albeit, as you say, into injury time
and you nothing now but a spare wheel on pain's wagon —
abba, Father, tarry
for at least a few more measly Christmas cards

mother

and you were born out of the old gentleman's loins,
he of the upright torso waistcoated and watch-chained,
the town-going fedora and glasses swimming with soft eyes:
among farmer folk who kept an ample but penniless homestead
where the first mountains encyst their solitude,
the Sandveld, dune world (visions of white harvest fields
with cool bluegums tokening rest) in the company of them
who burr their consonants because they love one another
and the grace of the sea: Struisbaai, Stilbaai, Spoelbaai, Dansbaai,
where strange treasures wash ashore: kists of marbles, copper
bedsteads, books, jars of balm, dead predicants, crosses, sextants
and curvaceously carved bowsprit nymphs from another hemisphere;
the sea of grace
where you will never know whether waves have eyes of laughter
or tears, and each rainbow drags its veil thick with rain:
(southsayer, say, which is more blue: the mountain sky,
sea shimmer, or my grandpa's speck-bespectacled eye?)

impoverished, his house? no, even though he humbly lay down roads
of pebbles and sand for the Divisional Council,
           his house was a haven melodious with names:
Sebastiaan, Rachel, Johannes, Bettie, Schalk, Martha, Anna,
Bert and Susanna and right on till daybreak; there was the quadrille
and the polka, squeezebox and mandolin, music for Africa;
on their charitable erf they cultivated their own bullrush
and broombush, sorrel and marigold and heather and laughter;
from the sea's recesses come *alikruikels, perlemoen,*
harders, kabeljou;
trees were heavy with sun; in the larder *konfyts* and meats and meal,
in the kitchen pancakes and honey
from those bee-filled graves, so the blossoms grow;
and nights when the moon rides down every cloud,
and other nights when stillness rolls from horizon to horizon,
the Southern Cross smoking in its cradle, Orion, Rigel, Betelgeuse,
Procyon, Aldebaran, Sirius, Eridanus, Antares, Canopus, Arcturus,

Eastern Cross, Centaurus the clod of gold
and other star-branches a-crackle and a-smoulder . . .

and he died and was gathered in among his fathers,
he died like glassed eyes toppling from the bedside table,
he died and went to bloom a few fathoms deep,
blossoming twigs massed with galaxies, graves topped with sweetness:

                    and you,
I grew up under your skirts;
when I think of you I see shy cheeks and plaits,
an apron full of flowers and a green sun hat:
I never know if you're laughing or crying ('oh rubbish!'
you snort), and I smell the warm sea-vulnerable earth
and cinnamon and cloves and flowers: snapdragons, *kalkoentjies*,
larkspurs, roses, swordlilies, *perdeklou*, pansies, zinnias,
magnolias, *uiltjies*, frangipanis, *bobbejaantjies*, gardenias,
poinsettias, pig's ears: your tongue gives pollen and petals
and bees, yes, you speak flowers, you heal what hurts,
you bind the rain in a spell of light;
I hear you hum at the harmonium
and see how you turn the shadows blue; the sea-breeze nestles
in your hair, a small ruby flickers on your finger;
for you the fullness is created at the back door
and all the world throbs out front
always brimming with delight: ah, life swift as the flick
of a wrist and your hands are never still; butterflies of love
hover above your head:

and now you are old, saturated with love and young for ever
like a fruit tree in the soil:
I bear your bones your careening blood
and the sing-song sounds of your throat:
oh mother, bless me before you go!

the wake

when my mother was dying
I had to flay my way through the seething current
to reach the bedstead where they had laid her out
in the yard: sparkling yellow
the sun stroked the arcadian scene
playing up the choir of ancient faces of extinct
uncles and forefathers sitting peacefully
sucking pipes to warble smoke,

strong and chipper she was under the white sheet
her eyes luminous and somewhat surprised without the spectacles
her plumpish arms distributing with deliberate gestures
the ultimate messages and blessings
(only the tired grey bun had already come undone):
visions of everything going swimmingly and she
at rest now with *interalia* Matthew and Mark left and
right the two old geezers were by Jove standing to,

and she also kept on beckoning me by the name
and could not place me at all,

but I had to retrace my steps lest the authorities
get wind of my escape into the current's
quickening whirl I sank
(was this the great drowning?)
to wash up teeth a-chatter lower down between banks
somewhere past farmlands where mud-spattered
grain elevators slash the heavens where haystacks
rot and turnips are gorged down by the turf,

and straining at their leashes I heard the stinking
dogs their throats clogged with the yelping fury of the hunt

in the days of the prophets

in days of the prophets when seers still crowed over the land
and life all one white bread, no husked breath or claudication,
the wind blue, white-horsed lovers high-stepping
with Saturday-night quiffs brilliantinting the moon – then,
you say, you too saw the man who wore his hair to the waist
and slept summer and winter huddled any which way
where thick lizards slip silvery between tumbleweed and heath

he could see the future taking form like the hair of the present
foretelling pleasures in a fragrant fashion, panting
at the brooch, molasses, ruby on *kukumakranka*-shy finger, marzipan,
and the marvels flowing from the honey-moon, that winter
is divestment but with luck buds may soon knot handkerchiefs
to the stripped branches – and then? did he say
the pain expelled through some deeper furrow into life?

foothills evening haze the years came to fire and ash,
and standing your ground you kept the seasons too,
fire chariots towers of smoke and mayhap manna twilighting flowers
so you would have to face the dawn with dreambread in your eyes,
but what the sower had sowed the maggot was to come and reap:
did he say anything of crows encircling darkness
when republics die, of skeletal winds over a yawning farmstead?

nothing? death comes so intimately and you now just the honey
for another lover's bread – my time-and-times love, my times-ago beloved
hanging loose of bowel and limb in the bush of bitter vowels –
I will remember the old-age blotches, the shoes worn skew, the jaws
too slack to chew rancid rinds, and tonight my eyes again choked
on the moon straying in the waste: true that winter loots the world
though buds may yet knot handkerchiefs to the stiffened branches

phylogeny

with the rains the winter comes
slinging dead words from the sky
the mornings are sombre stained books
leafed over page by dark page
slithering through the two thumbs

naked vineyards now the pointing fingers
                              of the blind
each message and remembrance untranslatably soft
the mirrors of day wrinkle away in water –
you turn over the soggy memory
to find comprehension with worms writing a face

beyond the muddy tumescences
further than puffed bellies and budding hands
the dreamt ones lay all dreamt away
sunk into the great ever-change
brought about by winterknow

mornday tumpternoon and humped night
a green moonmoth swerves
                              with the glitter of quartz
and in the nocturnal afterbirth of blue sculpthours
the snake with the cold shivers of its eyes
its flailings in mire also without sense

paradise-garden gardens of decay
images hungering for fulfilment
                              tongue through the verse
till an I corrupted to blindsight
                              with language-fouled eyes
again try by the magic maggots of phonemes
                              to sing together
the whole absence

consolation? that somewhere spring comes quivering
from the wetsay sods and that seed
must first decompose to burst and point?
no, rather that all deliquesce to flowing and to flux
in the darkness of dark multiplication

thus without the dead the living cannot read
the pretty syllables slung from heaven
with rain the many winters come

watching over the wall

first the total blue cupola
then a frayed white cloud pure white
the white and single dream
of a very old man with mangy memory
who in his day
so much liked the night butterflies

then the half-circle moon
very white in this day
a calvity with old age stains
the white speckled baldness of a very ancient
rotten cheese man
wading through deep waters

and higher than enclosures a butterfly
whitely frolicking
one at first then two floppily annotating
white flight two white kerchiefs one
in an invisible train

every day is wedding

the truth

geynest under gore,
herkne to my roun —

do you still remember when we were dogs
how we used to trot
on little pawed sores
through the tunnels and sluices of the town
streets of flapping yellow sheets
across cobblestones mud dykes loose planks
and leafy avenues
canals which even the rats never explored
do you remember how low we were against the ground
and how exhausted we grew
with flabby bloodlimp rags for tongues
from panting hard up the hill
right through hedges glass walls concrete shafts
past fearsome knots of streets with their spurting traffic lights
foundations drains cellars and cesspools where the heel-
jerks of the hung dead still adorned the breeze
with day and night but a drooping of the eye

till we arrived at the house of old Master R
where we could eat and smoke and drink
vodka for me and *tchai* for you
and sugary cookies for us both

and our grasp of the city
no one else could know
that it was in reality
a rhythmic intertwining flow

do you still remember when we were dogs
you and I, best beloved?

Isis

1

'l'amour est mort de trop d'amour'

you concentrated on what's on the table.
in the dark (I) can't make it out.
lean over your shoulder and see:
you busy fitting out a jigsaw puzzle
piece by piece:
the pattern takes form (I) see:
my portrait, my outline, me!

your hands agile (rats)
your connoisseur's eye
so thorough behind half-closed lashes instincthiefly
you know how to fill (in) the gaps

and now? you stand up
(a few spatters of egg on the sheet)
while the most sombre fragment/
the central bit is (still) absent

one:
don't for god's sake leave me lying this way incomplete
as the late lamented upon his bed! or

two:
no, rather don't ever round me out, love. build always alone
to that point where I remain part of you, reader.

'oh my love, my darling, I hunger...'

when your hand caresses me once more
do it carefinger carefully
remember I am no longer whole
pieces are gone patches scorched
with the years the other's share
scabbed over sore the envelope is rough
is dully reduced to torse
with limbs and the logic chopping
of nerve motives

dim like ice
with acerbity of smoke in fibre and membrane
through pucker and crack deceased
up to the deadened epiderm

for too long have I forgotten
the deft tips of fondling
the flower fingering of dalliance
woven in arabesque in hiprock and tapis

perhaps you should steal a wing somewhere

we must go begging borrowing
a crumbled totality
frayed to the ultimate strophe
we must venture over the hard rind
of frozen waters behind
the mirror dolphins tress a playful parabola
somewhere profoundly tip and tuck
and meanwhile so dark
how everything in the dark dips and ducks
half a life prawn plankton krill
predacious fish seal eel also rotten carcasses

of discovery barques sunk
so clear
clear it must be to plunge through a flaw
in the white-word-floe surface
plumbing down deeper the healing
oblivion, *whole*
when your hand writes me all over again

jantra

many a year the mountain's not been as green
such a proud sparkling gem
as in this early panoply of dying;
it is the passage to segregation –
autumn squandered its riches in burnt hues
and the force of renewal slumbers
lifelessly curled on Sesha's coils –
and yet each day is pure and still
so that the most shell-sheltered particularity
with a brightness bringing to mind life
stands clear from full to overflowing
crest unto the furthermost chime
under sun's shiny cicatrice

with peaks ever more fair under mourning snow
my beloved along the mountain passes we'll go
up to the hips in white oblivion
and from the coldest and sharpest-toothed summit
hand in hand (since together we feather wings)
wu wei wu wei fearlessly plunge
a fall endlessly away to the fertile god-patched valley
now so long greening ago

(Vesak, 1981)

your letter

your letter is delightful, larger and lighter
than the thought of a flower when the dream
is a garden,
        as your letter opens
there is an unfolding of sky, word from outside,
wide spaces,

I slept in green pastures
I lay on the ridge of the valley of the shadow of death
during the last watch of the night
listening to those condemned to die
being led through tunnels in the earth,
            how they sing
with the breath at their lips
as residents at the point of leaving
a city in flames, how they sing
their breaths like shackles,
          how they sing
they who are about to jump from light into darkness
they who will be posted to no destination,
terror fills me at the desecration,

the table before me in the presence of my enemies
is bare, I have ash on my head,
my cup is empty,

and I fled to your letter to read
of the orange tree decked out in white blossoms
opening with the sun,
I could smell it on the balcony,
           I can smell you
lovelier and lighter than the thought of a flower
in this dismal night,

I will be suspended from the sky of your words,
give that I may dwell in your letter
all the days of my life,

envoi,
your letter is wonderful, larger and lighter
than the thought of a flower when the dream
is the earth of a garden,
                              as your letter opens
there is an unfolding of sky, word from outside,
memory,

mon amour
            this I is dead
with green of blowflies at eyes and mouth
but from the *hara* of this silent tumulus
through bolted gates and barred apertures
further than the walls of the fort
and road-blocks and ditches and dikes around the settlement
behind the reluctant hills and the shifting desert
beyond the rain forest's rustling
running to the flickering of the sea
I see you/I talk you
                    mon amour

in the golden city of Rome
in that gilded cemetery I saw you waiting
my eyes your mouth full of pearls
and the rooks of your hair in my mouth
you stand like a *Cupressus funebris*
I saw your skin mirroring the sun
the shield of a brave little warrior
the mound of a valiant little tortoise

and when the fear arose
ah and when the unease of another continent
deposited its eggs in your eyes
maggots worming for the heart
I saw you take flight
first past Civitavecchia then higher along the coast
with red houses draped in washing pine copses
against the slopes tunnels disgorging
the whistling of trains
and vineyards and date palms groping for the sea
Genoa, a frontier...

beloved well-beloved
a blind Heterocera your blotted anguish at night's pane
and in Nice, Provençal waif,
among the shades of holiday-makers
your eyes turned South from whence
no news will reach you now
I felt you flinching
you so strong, you so weak

the man you're waiting for
will no longer be this I
but older, like winter snow in the cracks
old like a wounded wind from the interior
and he will carry me back with him

will you wait for us?
don't mourn do
stay the way I see you now
keep our time in your hands your mouth
safeguard our joy destroy our pain thus
remain: a festive territory for my dreams ...

for you're the warmth of my hand-palms the stones
of my dates the hairbreath hesitations of my deeds
the breath of my lips

ah mon amour
> look, I'll return
> and till then all
> over this horizonless page
> I write sightless write tongueblind towards you

the riding song of the bridegroom

when it's *moussem* again in Imilchil
and the Imazighen come down
from black frowns and folds of the Atlas mountains
to barter sheep for salt and seed
I shall load my sly donkey with tent-ropes and mats
twist paradise dreams in the lengths of my headcloth
with a white tongue in the neck
to show you how eager I am
for love
and legs astride legs astride ride through the gorge

when it's *moussem* again in Imilchil
where the many tents cower like great seagulls spreading
wide their wings around the sweet mausoleum of Sidi Mohammad el
    Merheni
panting for a breeze from the mountain heights
I'll come looking for you
amid the wreathing bee-bodies of marketers

look for your black eyes your veiled voice the whispering
flow of your silhouette
I wish to decipher the gimp of the lining of your hand
please let me buy you your bridal gown

my mountain gimmer my desert fruit
when it's *moussem* again in Imilchil
I'll know you from the kohl around your eyes the carmine
on your cheeks the cape of woven colour over the bride-white robe
and around your throat the clouds of happiness and my good fortune
in silver and amber and bud-in-glass
for you have taken hold of my liver

the *marabout*'s honey is a thesis in dust
you will rub a handful over your white-seamed breasts
to exorcise winter's pale nights with summer

and the pollen of bees —
I shall pay the *qadi* my ransom money
and free of bygones and state and tribe
let my dust lie down intimately with yours

tonight we'll roast the *mechoui* over embers of the vine
and nibble at the fat sheep's white eye with our teeth
the juicy udder and the mountain oysters
tonight we'll roist hump-backed by the ululating wail of the flute
around flames flickering closer and clearer than the stars

and when the earth has turned...
come return with me to my eternal bed of snow
behind white fortress walls on the roof of the day
where the fig tree mutters its royal shade in recitations
and pomegranates are golden cheek-mirrors against the slopes
where the heart of the well figures deep black water
that you may hoodwink me with the rock-rocking of seasons
and teach me how blossoms flower the whole year through

because you took possession of my liver —
be the staypole of my tent my mountain fruit my desert gimmer
let me strip the bridal finery from your tattooed sweetroot-bush
and legs astraddle without saddle ride to heaven through the cleft

like the wheel

(a squib)

when Mohandas K. Gandhi was still in South Africa,
a good man, loving his neighbour and others as well,
he sported a hat, elegant, dark grey, perhaps
a Homburg; and a starched collar,
necktie, waistcoat, lace-up boots: the works —
and the eyes were wide and somewhat squidgy
as if he surmised the whole world
to be contained within that camera
(around him one sees little indication
of coolies in the sugar plantations
of waving green waves all the way down
to where sari-blue waves begin to waver)

later the Mahatma was squeakier, fluted
and more like a mynah, on his nose perched
the perky colonial spectacles of learning
permitting him to perceive the tip of his nose,
the upper and lower parts of his face
two wobbly hubcaps without wheels,
and not really very much in the way
of squeamishness needing to be covered by the dhoti
(quite another cup of tea this sub-continent
a pullulation of pacifists paralysing
British Administration — with in the background
also pom-pom-pom and ratatatat
and swordslashes and Sikhs with sesquipedalian
blood sashed around their heads:
spoils will not be easily disgorged)

later still, going down to the waters,
having fastened his teeth for too long in fasting,
and he too brittle now like a thread of flax
around the spinning-wheel, when the zealot

hailed him — he turned to squelch himself
squandering upon the blade of nakedness
the flash in the sun as from an eye crutched,
or was that the squiffy bird vomited forth
from its dark chamber?
thereupon bashful red, fire, spices,
smoke squiggling like spiralled prayers et cetera.

— naked on starkers off —
by his cowl will you know the monk,
by its beak the bird
(one wonders whether in that last spasm-count
of leave and stocktaking he also saw the wind
once more blueing the slopes of the Drakensberg)

minotaur

thing earthed in its own nature has neither wish
nor want for more nor remorse: dark rose;
man severed from his earthing is history alone
heaped up shaping him, no better to come worse
nothing but the scree of the past — whatever is witnessed
is instantly doomed to oblivion, consciousness
drifts by swamped and swamped again,
even the circular path begins to spiral

where then was the garden of Hassan-i Sabbah
extolled 'Master of the Mountains'?
        Qasr Khan: near Alamut, his tight-lipped stronghold
where he would have young acolytes smoke hashish
and lead them through the night along paths of narcosis
to a secret garden (in this barren tongue of land?)
with pearling flowers and beheaded silver fountains:
houris and beautiful boys stroking instruments till they shivered,
eyes lined with kohl and their loins with moon,
bringing platters of dainties, jars purple with wine
for the guests, upon smooth-swinging hips:
dark rose

'this is the vision of Paradise
which you will return to (dead or alive but one
single name) when you've seen to it that my enemies are slain'
says Hassan

and each star-by-star humble herdsman of the hills
tries to round out the ring of his life:
times fruit in the cup, moon on the knife
of the assassin:
the rose dark

caught in the cold snows of a dream

Snow falls thick flaked in my sleep
and white the coast and white the sea,
inhospitable, a dismal trudge
through scourmarks, rustle and crunch, hatched strokes.

Of grey cement
the deserted towns,
of grey cement the streets and trees
all hung with droplets
like small microphones
intercepting the greyness to make it loud.

Our neighbours are in the gurgling of water-pipes,
hairy window-panes, eyelashes
over the wet of the iris. Into
the white eye of your layman-body
I will descend. Your teeth are tiny snowmen.
I will diminish in the lens.

There are sentries
with black tongues, tongues
like the pustulant moon, and silver
machine-guns
in the neck between the torn sea
and the bottomless snowfields of the interior:
a border post

on paper

In days of yore it must have been a voyage to the tacking
limits of the breath – picture it: the rakish vessels
groping along the outlines that stretched the maps
to their current shape, flowing round, worrying the charts of knowledge,
on permanent lookout for any coast of sorrow to leeward,
and then, white bit in the teeth, into the blue.
The deck stoned white and caulked thick with oakum
dancing-dancing under a man's feet, the future yet to be written
(and here already parameters and meridians of Turk,
Biscayan and other brigands).
Ennui much of the time (seagulls powdered wigs upon the waterway),
but under the surface the uncertainty whenever guidelines waver,
that man and mouse might turn to mutiny
out of terror for the dragon of the deep,
that your shaky skills as chirurgeon or woundmaster
might hold no sway over bloody flux or scorbutus,
and when the wind begins to bloom (excitement budding too)
through mainyards and rigging and jibs and backstays,
dragging at boom and gaff till the mizzenmast flexes
and below the bowsprit the figurehead *con le tette al vento*
lifting and falling with a shudder against the green slope of water,
and worse – picture it: an *orencaen*,
the barque bursting from her joists
like a well-endowed dowager from the whale-bone of her stays;
there is sploshing in the bilges, scupper-holes clear their throats,
bulk-heads split, a leaky hatch, shrouds ripped to rags, the cleats
had better hold and you're forced to cling to the capstans
or lose all control and be washed overboard –
wondering if the pumps will bail out the scum
and if your load of passengers is going to stand
for supping off lurching plates;
you might even be cut off from your corpse
were you to suffer a human fate.

There is no need to speculate: history is a one-eyed volume.
We know he crossed the Line
and one day softly breathed out upon a becalmed exotic
coast of green, came bobbing into a cove or bay
where the hook would not drag, and set his people,
grown oldish for lack of fresh vegetables, free
to go ashore.
The rest is stale news.

In the service of the Generale Vereenighde Nederlandtsche
G'octroyeerde Oostindische Comp. trade is plied
in the East, from Deshima Station in Nagasaki Bay.
He is ambitious, cunning but not necessarily underhand
(an admirable trait to be passed down as cultural heritage),
and so as to reach the highest goal he sets sail in due course
for other lands –
joins up with fellow mongers and sharpshooters, to visit Catsiou
(present-day Hanoi) and diverse settlements in Quinam
(Annam, surely), even learns to read and write the 'Tonkinse *taal*'
(as Western barbarians of the time knew Vietnamese)
and clinches a deal with one Mandarin Trinh Spiderbeard
for five and twenty kists of silver.

Things always run awry. There is the whiff of fraud.
In the year 1645 to top it all an *extraordinarien tuffon* comes
wrecking the mulberry trees and pushing flat the warehouses:
when leaves fall the silkworms come to grief
                    and books are worn threadbare.
Seeing as how the entire Indies rule is beset with the pestilence
of private commerce, he is declared *inter alia* unfit to serve
(edicts to this effect are promulgated) –
now there, one might say, is a fly in the ointment
to be caught, company jack, with your paw in the pot.
Under such a cloud of suspicion he departs from that land of spices
and love, perhaps takes leave also of his heart,
in the end – after some sort of puerperium –
to be demoted to commander of a roadside tavern
in the white margin of another, blackguarded continent.

(Arrived here lord of stormy petrels, chained convicts, thieves
of honour, mercenaries and other such *glücksritter.*)
(And that is where I come into the picture.)

Not far from where the jail lies now
at the Cabo de boä Esperance a colony is founded
which is going to lead to seasons and centuries of bitterness and grief.
I mean: if only that breath had puffed us past
this paradise of wretchedness and etched us stark
        as fishbones in Antarctica!
And yet in the smelting down, the crucible's bastard fusing
begins a smoothishness, raw pain's fresh metamorphosis –
and how could it really be otherwise? – out of all those noses
and arseholes and arteries and ovaries of assorted nations,
those Nederlanders, Engelschen, Franschen, Hoogduitzers
(of many regions), Savoyaards, Italiaanen, Hungaaren, Maleyers,
Malabaaren, Cingaleezen, Javaanen, Macassaaren, Benjaanen,
Ambioneezen, Bandaneezen, Boegineezen, Bubineezen, Chineezen,
Madagascaaren, Angoleezen, inhabitants of Guinea
and of the Zoute Eilanden,
all of them using the Nederduitze, Maleitze and Portugeesche tongues,
new blood will come.
Wind. Paper.

Now do you see how deep the troughs of history run
between your country and the one which is mine as well?
And do you realize why when I glance at a banknote
with the portrait of that hybridized 'founding father' –
jaunty wig and arrogant nose –
as a drifter I should think of you, and the strange
enchantment of silkworms?
because he too yielded to the rustling,
leaping head over heels into the unknown?

But you may well imagine, and that's the imprint of stale news
which hasn't yet fully dawned in the paper.

what counts

And so you wish to hear about my literary I-dolls?
Well, when Lorca was as old as I am now
he was long since wormturd and legendary shade,
Rimbaud's baited leg had already reeled
him to his hive,
And Mayakovsky since time immemorial had blasted
a telescope clean to heaven through his skull.
Which goes to show that they were perhaps wise
in the ways of the word
but knew sweet bloody nothing about keeping alive.

about the shadowline

when Mahakashyapa had decided that the moment
of his paranirvana was at hand, the final quenching
of the very breath and the breaking of the wheel
of rebirth, then his beloved disciple — thick
shiny skull and saffron robe — came to shoo
me to him, led me through a bearded tunnel
to a coast that knew neither kiss of waves
nor keel lipped in sand — glassy, bare:

there Kashyapa brooded like a brown sun
above the dusky hills and all his acolytes
bewailed his leaving with dust so that *he*
leafing through the sacred book had to console *us*,
thin words pale with mystery, but saying all,
also the jokes, and in tears he recalled the offspring
of French and Italian rulers over Yourip, a spring
of scoffing at the debauched titles in the annals

of history, their immorality, and how the dynasty
came to grief with a certain *fille de samedi après-midi* —
alas: the time was at hand, and on another page, ripped
from the future, he pointed out to us the diagram
of his successors already sketched, darkening star's
dotted life, names of those inheriting beanbowl
and *kesa*, from one to one, and who will know
how to cut out the flower of invisibility

to pass it along unpainted by words — only
the beloved at his knee was nowhere on that list
(how now? for in a shooting light interiorized
I could surmise already how the latter would anon
deny this denial of legitimacy and greedily usurp leadership)
and more, Kashyapa murmured, turning over again
to look at me — as for *you* and the winds,
look here, not in time but in space, step

by horizontal step, in an elongated parabola
obliterating my hunch and inking from there
like perfectly awakened tailfeathers pointing ahead
all behind you — do you hear the sun talking? —
you will be the first patriarch of a new school
of birds — the suchness stays and flies away — I say
you will have nothing to say, Bird the Silent,
only the transmission of nought — glassy and bare:

but how knowest thou that that spot be I, I
wanted to know — look, my name is not even
jotted in thy book; but no, he was not to mouth
a measly word in response, only mocked me
with a plastic smile and closed the pages — we knew
now that what he'd been waiting for,
the ash-moment, would flare and thus snap this
syllabic cord for him to plunge to *sunya*'s edge —

do scoop that earth out from under me, his voice
intoned — I feel a cloddishness under the blades —
and we started digging down; all is ash,
he continued: I cannot die, the knife of my life
has cut me out a prisoner, the light too strong!
and indeed, we dug, but where there should
have been down was only earth, till he — o miracle —
sank still alive and kicking into the empty mattress.

on the way to ku

at the pagoda all was in a stir:
the news did the rounds that Mahakashyapa
was lying in wake-wait for destruction
in the meditation hall
and in the gardens of vacuity
around the building
a throng of newshounds milled and mustered paraphernalia:
cameramen with -scopes and -meters
like metal fish with eyes soft guzzle-mirrors
in which a rainbow swims, soundmen with -phones
and -captors like rank bazookas or eavesdropping
storks;
in the vestibule itself the racket was infernal:
young bonzes haywiring uproariously beside themselves,
wolfing down *meat* yet and at times wanting to smuggle
in a whole haunch under the hem — explaining
that they dwell in the fourth dhyana, thus
the tremor of unbridled ecstasy
(but all these are but excuses and farce: the a-peripheral
circle gives way and all things collapse
to attachment)

'I'm so glad you could come' the old nun says —
'because he repeatedly called out for you
even though he doesn't know your name;
oy, and I'll *so* much appreciate it if you could
give him *this*, that he may *pray* for us,
and we be *blessed*,' and she gives me
the grey cone which fits over the hands
with the pagoda's name (and special requests)
embroidered in small rubies of blood on the hood — only then
do I notice the cupidity in her eyes

in there with him it is quiet
as ever, where he lies, stretchered, the eyes

two grey plovers with arched backs
and wings spread
to hatch black-black embers
so that nothing can be seen of the eyes,
only joss-sticks smoulder in the penumbra
the way each firefly hovers a glow around its sweet fire
of sweetness —
'lord!'
and he twists and turns, maroon and smooth
like an old rubber plant: the thought/borne mind
must while away
till just the haft remains ere
you can bite with that blade to the root

'lord! —'
then I hear him moan, that he cannot die
although the flock of lives have long since fled
the body
and he (present and gone with the wind) on every wing
beating its fragmented blue oblivion;
'perhaps it would help' I hear the rustling whisper
in the coop,
'if you could hold my head to the floor
while I go for an ultimate tumble'

'to live is to burn'

Andrei Voznesensky

all is luminous and all is still: to live is to be
digested like this summer-day of loveliness; ever
and again to praise the globe rocking by, the sultry leafage
of thickets, water-slips, stone-lips, the feathered ones' heart-chips
changed to chain-eyes linking silence to silence; how totally rich
the mountain, naked, sun-caked — only one plume whitening
the wind which soon must bulge slender organ-sounds
and streamers; and it is done, spiralling the cycle of seasons
has heaved old wrinkles like worms from the lap —
but look, we are each the coachman of oblivion, rigor mantis
with bleached hands at death-cart's reins. Prayer by prayer
our way is cocked, cool, a skeleton chaliced in day-dress of flesh ...

burn, burn with me, love — to hell with decay!
to live is to be alive, while alive to die anyway

smoking

already 72 months I've rooted in the winter
of a cycle that knows nothing but winter any more
and the fireless flame at passing time's core
the crackling rain the smooth cold
dogs left to lie pigs that will never fly

you don't need a weatherman
to know which way the wind blows —
black and icy it blooms out of a pool
of emptiness in the mask of Shiva
lord of all annihilation the passionless
dance/dancing the undanced dance
the fitful freezing together of life and death
in a single dignified quadrille of the heart

already all of 72 months the amnesiac disease
the rat endlessly spinning the treadwheel
the whitespout of want barren and ecstatic
seeking stopgaps for another's body
that other who must lose form rhythmically
the juggler's cold and flaming balls
sucked up in this timeslit's yawning loss

but with this cigar, Toscano, *extra-vecchio* . . .
I light up the leaf, ring out a code of smoke
and bring summer's husbandry to mind
where thrushes sing black cypress songs notched
note by note in the stucco of red walls
while a sun rich in hours is gushed out green
across the string of terraces planted with vines
the clock-tower and cupola of Florentine stone

what's dead is life as well —
wisdom the burrowing path impressed with ageing's
brake and boundary —

pictures? droplets that burn on in gutter and drain
the mountain outside still so stocky and sombre
and over the prisonpit Shiva's cold
black-scorched feet come trippling once more
with the passionate measure of all creation

another poem? throw the butt away –
the current will justly pay no heed to the leaf

liberation

here I am this first day already shimmering bright
among angel choirs: afar the feathered folk sing psalms
my face smells of beauty my hands are embalmed
did I not store the leftover oil for years
with precisely this meeting mirrored in mind?
very still I will lie holding in my glee
so as not to rock the earth on this last lap

dance, raise the dust beloved – why are your eyes so grey?
let friends pick sprays of laurel leaves
and twist green victory garlands all entwined:
no one should sorrow so that the bier may be becalmed
for I am yours now picked clean of all disgrace
where wind-softly dolphins orbit in the palms
yours entirely released in the gardens of the night

here we go

laybyes and gauntletmen, allow me to take this leave
of Bangai Bird,
the emaciated dream in the green shirt;
he props up and fondles his wormfat head
and breeds a final poem to bestow on you,
for example:

to come out of hospital you must
be in a coma
dead but wise to the light looming at your lids
how the shadowmoon swims!

run back from the sea
to the labyrinth of loneliness where the mountain
contracts round
the forest the trees are columns of darkness

run the delicate web of hurt
bird-heads tilting with silence gone to pus
dazzled by moon deep in egg eyes
and drizzle that never wets the dust

past neighbours clay dog barking a farmyard
sink to the knees in daze shout get away! shoo!
gaolers make an offer they'll ride on with you
but the motorbike sputters and stutters apart
bitter cunning ducks have pecked the outer body through
and the scrawl clots white
look the hands themselves rot

see, he is versed in harmfulness —
would you not rather show him mercy?
the feast of words has been consumed,
no one is guilty of innocence

22–11–1982

114

afterword

The foregoing poems are culled from a much larger number originally written in Afrikaans and in prison from September 1975 to December 1982, since published by Taurus Publishers, Johannesburg, in five volumes with the collective title of *Die Ongedanste Dans* (*The Undanced Dance*). Denis Hirson translated some and I was glad and grateful to be inspired by his versions.

Every poem has its own shape, (in)formed obviously by the language within which it lives, through which it moves. I believe, though, that this shape can be apprehended and clothed or unveiled in other tongues. The present volume is not a translation, but rather, as Octavio Paz would have it, a transformation into another language. Whether these verses would want to work in a new garb is a different story: some were weak from birth.

I have no intention of explaining. A poem is a merging of land, which may make sense, and sea which must be the irrational structured by movement and rhythm. This is no reason however for creating seasons of obstacles to the reading.

Afrikaans — ironically the only language on the continent to call itself 'African' — is a bastard tongue, as I've said elsewhere. It still bears clearly the traces of its origins: that marriage between sea, the slang of sailors and slaves from many regions, and the inland vernacular of settler peasants and indigenous peoples. It is sad and perhaps inevitable that one of the most mixed and mixed-up tribes of history should so much have wanted to adhere to the canons — biological, historical, political, linguistic — of a fallacious purity. Purity kills: first the Other and then the mind. Or the other way about, I'm not sure which.

The development of Afrikaans starting from when the white foreigners first picked up dust on the coast to precipitate and participate in the lengthy dismemberment and agony of cultures and ethics — soon they were to import further non-white displaced persons from other colonies — can be read as maps folding over one another, blueprinting memory, fading references to existent borders and roots.

The poem, 'on paper' (p.102) touches upon the above. It is based partly on Company documents of the time, and the writings of an early 'explorer', a Swedish botanist or somesuch who noted the diversity of

115

peoples living at the Cape and the many languages then spoken there. From these, too, Afrikaans was to grow through the adaptory dialectics of corruption and invention.

The 'founding father' was Jan van Riebeeck, a governor demoted to commander in the Dutch East India Company, employing also *glücksritter* (knights of fortune) and other *hoi polloi*. Among the dangers encountered at sea by the barbarians there could have been the *orencaen* (hurricane) or the *extraordinarien tuffon* (extraordinary typhoon). The population, apart from the indigenous tribes, included: *Hoogduitzers* (High Germans speaking High German as opposed to the Nederduitz, the Low German, of the Dutch); Dutch, English, French, Savoyards, Italians, Hungarians; *Maleyers* (Malaysians); *Malabaaren* (inhabitants of the south-western seaboard of India); *Cingaleezen* (Sinhalese); *Macassaaren* (from Macassar); *Benjaanen* (inhabitants of Banjarmisin in Borneo); *Ambioneezen* (from the island Amboina, today Ambon); *Bandaneezen* (from the Bandas); *Boegineezen* (coming from Bougie/Bugia, the present Bejaia); *Bubineezen* (from the Island of Little People); people from the *Zoute Eilanden* (Schouten Eilanden, off Dutch New Guinea). And all spoke a version of Dutch or Malay or Portuguese or Malay-Portuguese et cetera.

Personal history is also a sum of quirks. My private trips need no elucidation; in fact, out of respect for the reader it is advisable to keep the voice at the level of an indistinct mumble, and it is not always necessary for a word to be understood in order for it to have meaning. Ornette Coleman says about music that it is like talking, and 'you can say whatever you like, so long as you don't disturb the flow and logic of the conversation'.

Nevertheless, and because they reflect the language behind the language, the ongoing *métissage* and invention, I'd like to refer to some of the riches left to me by the ancestors: childhood words and some of the fabric of prison slang. Where land is a lap to the sea.

In the poems to my father and my mother (pp. 77 to 80) — familiarly we called them *Oubaas* ('old master') and *Ounooi* ('old missus') — you will find that people walk through the *veld* (literally meaning 'field' but indicating the non-cultivated countryside, our *sertão*) with their *velskoene* ('handmade rough shoes of untanned hide sewn without nails, thought to be first made by the Hottentots before the arrival of the white man' — Jean Branford, *A Dictionary of South African English*, Oxford University Press, Cape Town, 1980), where they may be concerned about the *khaki-*

bush (an obnoxious smallish shrub with a nasty smell, inedible and spreading fast over the land, believed to have been brought into the country during the Boer War by means of the British – thus *khaki*: horses' droppings, also known as Mexican marigold). If you were to visit the south-eastern coast you would discover many beautiful bays: *Struisbaai* (the bay of the grass huts), *Stilbaai* (Quiet bay), *Spoelbaai* (where there is a strong tow, a wash and a flow), *Dansbaai* (where holidaying farmers would dance until the stars were dizzy). From the sea there you could gather, and enjoy, the *alikruikel*, also known as *alikreukel*, *arikreukel* (edible mollusc, *Turbo sarmaticus*, and in truth it is related to the snail or the periwinkle), the *perlemoen* (*Haliotis* with mother of pearl shell; we know that *lemoen* is an inversion of the Dutch *meloen*, *melon* – thus 'pearl melon'?), the *harder* (South African mullet), the *kabeljou* (Cape cod, but the word must be from the French *cabillaud*, which is of a different kettle). Do have some *konfyt* for dessert (preserved or conserved whole fruit or large chunks in syrup), and then go and take a gander at the flowers outside: the *kalkoentjie* (the word means 'little turkey' but the flower is of the Iridaceae species), the *uiltjie* (*Moraea neopavonia*, though the word, 'little owl', is probably a corruption of *uintjie* or *uitjie*, 'small bulb'), the *perdeklou* (*Eriospermum brevipes*; the word says 'horse's hoof') and the *bobbejaantjie* (literally 'little baboon'; species of *Babiana*). With luck, and in the right season, you may smell and follow your nose to the *kukumakranka* ('Any of the species of *Gethyllis*: usually signifies their fragrant club-shaped fruit which are dried for scenting rooms or cupboards, eaten or infused as brandy.' Branford, op. cit.). Stay on in the country, become aware of your surroundings. You may get to know ('the coming', p. 50) of *consolidated land* and *appointed places* and *passbooks*. These terms relate to our apartheid history, to snitches of land stitched together to house 'endorsed out' Africans, to dumping grounds for the homeless and other 'surplus people', the exiles who had to carry and produce 'reference books' everywhere in the country.

And the road to prison is paved with social consciousness. You may as well start by reading 'december' (p. 19), 'prisoner' (p. 31), 'the long arm' (p. 42) and 'for Françooi Viljoen' (p. 52) to familiarize yourself with *boop* (prison) slang when you *do your bird* (your time). The warder, the 'screw', will be known as either *Boer* (generic name for warders, policemen, soldiers, by extension all Whites; means 'farmer') or *Ghostkeeper* or *philistine*. Your inmate will be a *mugu* (probably of Zulu origin), a *skebenga* or

117

a *skemuggel* ('skebenga' comes from the Zulu *isigebengu*, gang member, which in turn derives from the Afrikaans *bende* meaning 'gang' – see how we run in circles?) or a garden *bandiet*. If you cultivate a friend you have a *connection*. If the inmate is a special friend indeed he may be a *poophole pilot* (a homosexual). The old down-and-outers are known as *lallapipes* (Afrikaans 'lallapyp'; 'lalla' is to sleep: someone so poor he'd be living under a culvert outside). Those sentenced to be hanged are called *condemns*. At least they don't have to break their heads about a *suspended* (a previously suspended sentence). You will eat your *graze* (food) from a *dixie* (tin plate), and then smoke some *snout* (tobacco), or even *issue* (rotten tobacco doled out by the administration), before getting a move on with your *taxi-pads* (folded strips of cloth on which you waltz over the floor to shine on shine on harvest moon) and your *Brasso* (cleaning fluid for copper). When you are really outraged you may try *standing on your dig* (dignity) (to stubbornly shout for justice). When your time for leaving finally approaches, you may scout the newspapers and find there's still *mahala graft* ('mahala' – Sotho for 'nothing'; 'graft' – work) outside. But go, for God's sake go! And as you go we'll wish you a heartfelt *hamba kahle* (Zulu greeting: 'go well').

All this then, and more, as part of my rag-bag of riches.

my heritage

'your grandpa'
says my father resting
before the light at the window
his head a dark songbird snared
in the oversized collar
'your grandpa was a farmer

'not all that – er – successful
since he went ploughing and planting
in never-never land and was hardly – er –
dexterous with his hands
but *peu importe*

'in the old days night fell anyway
before anyone could choose his way

'his farm ran down the Fish River
(ah I see again the banks buttocking
steep and lush and blue before me)
but he was a profoundly god-carrying man
a Buddhist – er – or of some other
obscure creed

'Sundays his house teemed black with prayer-people

'with his hands deep in the good clods
your grandpa
died of poverty
but *this* – er – and *this*
he left to you:'

with his voice my father reaches for
and caresses the heavenly spheres
and the sun a hill on fire

mountains with their rumpled cheeks clean acres
flowers humankind even canes wound
with snakes

: *'all this priceless dictionary!'*

SELF-PORTRAIT/DEATHWATCH

A Note on Autobiotrophy

I/Other. I don't find it pleasant to be turning over the leaves of myself, and yet I'm doing so all the time. When I describe an onion on the tablecloth I am detailing the self. God did not make this world, I did – conceiving the vibrant thoughts, the rolling hills, the scattering shadows, the holes in the ground, the ants, including God. How do you know my thoughts are not hills? Worse, I am still creating it and I may stop at any moment.

Why is it unpleasant then? Because consciousness is open-ended and subject to constant change and it is frightening, if not perilous, to keep on caressing the unknowable I. The hidden nature of awareness is that it cannot be stilled for long enough to be defined, not even temporarily like the dead person. If I do thus write about some id or other oddment it must be dead. Therefore I cannot write *about* me; I could only write I. And immediately the writing is blanched, staunched. Becomes *it*. The fly in amber. God in his grave. The ants will not go hungry. Writing as a weak form of awareness, a minute manifestation of movement.

It would be more illuminating to trace the trajectories of Panus, Elephterià, King Fool, Don Espejuelo, Geta Wof, Jan Blom, Vagina Jones, Lazarus, Comrade Ekx, Afrika Aap, or Bangai Bird ... To get *you* at the tip of my pen and/or into the word processor: I the Other or/and the other Other. Or to be free to create the third persons. It would indeed have been more than satisfying to paraphrase the true immortal self as Pier Paolo Pasolini, as Frantz Fanon, as Bertolt Brecht, as Billy Bodyday, as Matrice Mulumba, as Gueux Guevara, as Pablo Picasso, as Ho-Ho Hinh, as Manet Magritte, as G. Goya, as Fou Fu ... But the commission is to briefly sketch the public one in flux and in flop, the orator, the poet. Also, I assume, to point in passing at those of us – all but one – who fell dead by the roadside or gloriously died on the bridge – which translates as this and that about the past. And in this way to create history. History is the mother of invention. It protrudes and it is concave. It is open-minded. It is stained by the dead weight of what you have lived through, but it also delineates the absence of what you did not experience. I shall write about this you in order to duck the blame, to shift the weight, to sculpt the breathing space. The mathematically immaculate conception, then, of the mask known as Breyten Breytenbach.

Young/Old. In the beginning there is the verb. I was born many many years ago in a small town called Bonnievale in the south-western region of a state then still known as the Union of South Africa. (In 1961 it became the Republic of South Africa and still later, after a prolonged race war which pitted the least contaminated sectors of the Third World against the Western Democracies, it was to become the People's Republic of Azania.) My parents were of poor peasant stock. I had a twin brother who died at birth, and three more brothers and a sister. My mother passed away and was buried in the hills above the sea at the time when I was doing my apprenticeship to freedom as a political prisoner; if you were to cock an ear you might yet hear her laughing there. My father is alive and well and living in South Africa, even though he stopped talking more than four years ago.

As in other 'new' countries with like stories of conquest and colonialism, South Africans too would move from town to town and from job to job in an attempt to escape the taste of failure. In similar patterns my people navigated over the face of the Boland – the 'Upper Country', a radius of 200 kilometres from the Cape of Good Hope, the ancient grazing grounds of the now extinct Khoi people – and the bordering areas. It is without the tiniest bird of doubt the most beautiful land in the world. In the back of my mind there is even now the green motions of the two oceans.

When I was young I was intelligent. I went to school and subsequently to the University of Cape Town to study Fine Arts and Letters. I had already started painting and writing poetry to express my infatuation with loss and my exquisite sensibility. There were many flying foxes in the fruit trees. I would gradually learn and unlearn the adjectives. Then I dropped out of university to become a drifter – a creator, I fondly thought. I was on my way to satori. Little did I know that it was also the jump into a free fall away from the strictures of my tribe – which would yet leave me with the scar tissue of structures. I was going into the wide wide world, entering the many homes of exile, ultimately to be purged by poverty and prison and to become familiar with the poetry of politics.

Now I am old and facing a Chinese landscape shifting into focus and then forgetting itself: like a dream fading into memory, a thought washed away in shades of pale ink. Rather be verb than verbal, I say to my autobiographer. (Or verbose.)

Black/White. Calvinists hold to the dogma of predestination. Essentially it means coming to terms with being part of God's embroidery. It means, I think, accepting the salutary relief of fatalism. It also implies assuming that there is an *order* to life, to all that quiver and copulate in the celestial spheres and down hither — even down into the past or into the murky subconscious which, of course, is the passage to India discovered by Christopher Freud. This order has its temporal translation. Our terrestrial masters have the God-given *right* to rule and the interests of the State are paramount. (The State is God incarnate among men.) Many roads lead to totalitarianism, the power malady, but the above conception constitutes, I dare believe, a short cut to the priorities of law and security, to the inviolability of property, to the entrenched privileges of the strong; to holy wars, capital punishment, torture, whiteness and charity.

Threaded through the oriental approach to life is the belief in karma — or the legacies of that teaching, or the vital positioning *vis-à-vis* and interaction with the past and present histories of people holding to that belief. Hinduism and Buddhism also have their bodies of laws and customs — given half a finger the pious acolytes will go on droning for ever to embroider the obscurantist mind — but karma at least confers individual responsibility and it allows for the breaking of the wheel, the waking up from the coma of cause and effect. The Way makes the Law irrelevant.

I was born in a state where the white/black order was immutable. It warped all of us because even when we revolted against the tyranny of Apartheid — the maiming of the social body and the private mind — it was like in a shadow play in order to have one orthodoxy displaced by another ... I was born white (we are now talking of bureaucratic arbitration, tribal superstitions and ideological genetics, not nature), immediately a member of the master race, growing up under the signs of chlorosis. But as I started backing into the inner reaches of expanding consciousness I realized that my heart was black. You could say my heart is a night-club for the printer's devil. And it is the abjuration of the denial of my humanity, this unending trip towards integration, that I try to trace by the leucorrhoea, the *fluor albus* of my writing.

And I am convinced that life, as also the definitions by which we attempt to immobilize it (understanding is death), is an infinite and goalless process of metamorphosis — posited though, I should bloody well hope, on the meticulous search for jumps and breaks. The lion's roar

125

explodes the jackal's mind. In terms of social arrangements the 'jump' would be a revolution, a breakthrough to the suspension or the obliteration of pairs and opposites.

I may still be a bird or a horse or a stone. It is also not a bad idea from time to time to open the hole and pass down some embroidery or acupuncture needles to God; it is damp in the subconscious, one risks contracting rheumatism of the articulations there, and repeated movements may grease the joints. Perhaps I should not forget the pen and paper.

African/European. I realize that my expectations, my apprehensions, my instinctive recognition of *the right position and place* (read for this, if you wish, the unquestioned sense of security, of belonging), the means by which I experience space and rhythm and structure or the way of my relationship to the environment and to other people, my notion of breath and/or breathing space which flows from mountains and a cloud very high in the sea-coloured sky, that which reverberates as 'blue' in me if you were to utter the sign, as in blue like a coffin – that this substratum which constitutes the mechanism of my being was formed during the tender pre-rational years in Africa. I am an African.

There is in me the bedrock which can never be non-African. And then I was to become European too. I first arrived in Lisbon after travelling fourth class in a swinging hammock down in the hold of a liner which dropped anchor in all the Portuguese African ports. Black stevedores were at that time still driven along with whips. They weren't really black; their skins had a sickly grey pallor. Off the Cape Verde Islands we shipped more voyagers who sat in the bows the whole day long, singing sad songs and staring at the emerald waves to see the sun plumb the depths. I was twenty years old with pipe and beard and rucksack and twenty British pounds in my pocket. It was the European winter of 1960.

Then in South Africa there bloomed the massive campaigns of resistance to Apartheid, led by the Pan-Africanist Congress (PAC) and the African National Congress (ANC) – culminating in a chain of bloody repression with the Sharpeville massacre as its apotheosis. The black nationalist formations were banned, so too the South African Communist Party. People went into exile or entered the prisons. Nelson Mandela set out on his long walk to freedom, his dead life, his martyrdom. Abroad I got to know and sympathized and started collaborating with my militant compatriots, patriots all.

I had been to Spain where I made the acquaintance of Mr Goya with the silvery pants and the rosy buttocks and the black bowels. The Guardia Civil still wore patent leather hats as if acting out some Lorca poem, and they stank of death. In the Jura I got singingly pissed on home-brewn liqueurs and in London on dark beer. I worked on farms and stations and in factories, just long enough to qualify for the dole; I taught English in Bergen which was buried under snow, and earned one plate of food a day as a portraitist in a night-club in Nice. Sidney Bechet's 'La Petite Fleur' was the jukebox hit. I worked on a yacht in the Mediterranean and took part in a mutiny in the port of St-Ives. I slept under bridges and on vacant lots and near Hamburg in some rustling orchard and on the road to Newcastle curled up in the snow on the back of a 'donkey' used for heating an adjacent greenhouse. There was a white cat and I thought it must be the soul of my mother trying to speak to me in Afrikaans. I thought she must have died, but she continued writing to me via the American Express. With fellow bums I'd take my turn to warm a grey-sheeted single bed in some sleazy hotel room. And in an ancient sector of Paris I met Lady Lotus. We ran off to be married and for many years survived on the income from her salary. Vietnamese dishes became my favourite food.

In 1964 I started publishing in Afrikaans. Poetry and prose. Robert Rimbaud had disdainfully turned down my pleas to become my master. I'd continue publishing Afrikaans works right through the sixties and the early seventies, then take a break and start again during 1983. Extracts would later be translated into several tongues and eventually I was to start doing my thing in English and French. I painted in small rented rooms or in other people's studios and started exhibiting the results. Some paintings were taken off the walls or had to be blocked out because of obscenity.

Those were the radical sixties. In South Africa a generation of black writing was wiped out; a generation of white writing won the freedom to be sodomized by the tribal authorities and the writers turned to Europe for intellectual sophistication and decadence as a face-saving device. In Paris I moved with Black Panther hijackers, with revolutionary Brazilians, Kurds, Greeks ... I frequented a few of the charismatic leaders who lived in the shadows. There would be assassinations, as of Henri Curiel by

French agents carrying out a joint Israeli–South African contract ... 'We' lost Chile and, for a while, Argentina and Greece; but 'we' won Vietnam, Laos, Portugal, Mozambique, Angola, Zimbabwe, Guinea-Bissau. 'They' killed Lumumba, Luthuli, Ben Barka, Martin Luther King, Mondlane, Guevara, Malcolm X, Amilcar Cabral ... The Russians nipped in the bud the Prague spring. The permanent nature of imperialist appetites became abundantly clear. Africa grew poorer. Gradually the pre-eminence of the late twentieth-century empire's capital, New York, emerged and it was obvious that we'd have to face and counteract all kinds of cultural stratagems. Bourgeois leftists to their horror suddenly discovered the Gulag and the totalitarian nature of most communist parties, promptly moved to the right of the political spectrum, shat all over Third Worldism and forsook philosophy for fiction. Central European existential anguish was to become the locus of politically engaged intellectualism. But that came later. First there was the *baroud d'honneur* of May 1968...

Europe made me a world citizen, but it also caused me to become more aware of my Africanness. Inevitably there would be the returns to Africa. For some time I even held a genuine Algerian passport. I came to identify more and more with the complex war of the Third World – against disfiguration, for dignified survival, for true autonomy, for alternative economic circuits. I realized that the privileged role ascribed to the Judaeo-Greek heritage when talking about 'civilization' was nothing but the prejudiced and partisan and faulty interpretation of later manipulators; that 'Western values' – the cloak of expansionism – occulted alternative sources: Chinese, Arab, African ... I saw that the definition of 'progress' was tendentious and that applying it meant opting for a terrible crunching power mechanism. I could not picture myself as a *white man*, not even in bastardized shape. I am an African bastard – from a continent where *métissage* is continually absorbed; Africa, the continent where the reality of metamorphosis is paramount, where you have the chance of seeing the simplest object transformed into a votive symbol or a still point of magic; where there is a humbleness traversed by flashes of extravagant glory like flowers suddenly bursting upon an arid landscape, and the innate knack to live on the zero horizon of survival; where people don't have either/or minds but nonetheless an effortless mastery of dialectics to make of it a joyful game of *trictrac*; where bourgeois values are nearly totally absent, or at least those power relationships based on possessions or exploitation, or at least that materialism linked to the profit motive only, incarnating – as in the West – a pathological need to dominate and to recover lost and innocent certainties; a continent allowing for *other* readings of art, its functions and that of the artist (often hereditary), for humour; where there is still such an infrastructure of humanism that Africa even now cannot really work up the necessary revulsion to spit out the abject South African whites. Africa, where the whores are not outcasts. Africa, as I said, where your worth is not painted by what you have – though a watch plated gold and a ghetto blaster could be things of awe and mirth – but by how you are. By what you do to and for others.

Interior/Exile. I have consistently rejected the conception of exile as debilitating, petrifying, self-pitying – and yet again, many of my ruminations have circled around the condition of absence: not being where I belong naturally. I have tried to show up the negative aspects and the positive acquisitions of being expelled from the tribal framework and then permanently living *elsewhere*. It is true that you not only live outside the social and physical environment where you could have functioned instinctively and completely, but that you must also accommodate the lack, the absence, the feeling of having been deprived of your normal expectations. There is some alienation involved here, a land-sickness, a hankering after booming breakers and the mordant wit of a drunken proletariat and ripe stars and the perfume of gardenias embalming the night on a darkened veranda. But elsewhere you survive, as if in compensation, with an accrued sense of adaptation; you get to inspect the inner lining of integration; you are given distance as a consolation prize and perhaps you gain perspective too; you experience at last the self as God hiding in his grave with the febrile dance steps and movements of meaning of the ant.

When I left my native shores early during 1960 I had no intention of heroically going into the suffering of exile. In fact, I gradually grew into absence without ever being able to solve the ambiguities of my state of suspension. Like the other locusts I also became an *habitué* of the Préfecture de Paris. It was only in 1973 that I was allowed to return 'home' for three months and then, as reported in *A Season in Paradise*, the trip turned out to be an effort to come to terms with my roots, to be finished with the business of youth. Unsuccessfully so, as soon became clear – or else I'm a recidivist – because my clandestine return during 1975 was also partly motivated by the private need to go beyond the contradiction of being

129

passionately involved with 'down there' whilst living happily abroad. Finally, after seven and a half years of lying in prison like a pulse beat in the heart of No Man's Land, that umbilical cord was cut. Thereafter I could continue, knowing that South Africa will always be the mother-prism and pain for me, as well as a luck and a daunting challenge to all of humanity to lift our dull eyes to a new horizon during this last part of the century. I was liberated to live my leftover life fully elsewhere. To move with the changes. To paint and to write. To see the sky come shrinking closer. To accommodate the unexpected death.

This 'non-involvement' is not at all to the liking of the maggots who live on the morally revulsed body of anti-Apartheid the same way others — cigar-chomping vultures and stripe-suited hyenas too — continue feasting off the beastliness itself. It is no use me saying I'm not an exile: people would insist on having their need for outrage and public evisceration and catharsis satisfied.

The diaspora of South Africans probably reinforced an important component of our struggle: internationalism — eventually also in the beneficial sense of Pan-Africanism and Third World consciousness and not only as socialist prattle — thereby saving it from being just another nationalist black uprising.

Free/Unfree. I am a statutory, convicted terrorist. This I am inordinately proud of although I realize how easy it is to become one in the perverted context of South Africa — where after all we find a population of 5 million albinos and 25 million actual or would-be terrorists. Our exclusiveness has been vulgarized, our mythological nature ridiculed! We are becoming as common as garden tourists!

I have covered many pages with reflections and speculations pertaining to freedom, as if covering my tracks. I have come up with quotable thoughts even if these were filched from someone else. Should one not be free to steal?

This concern with freedom evidently became more acute after my conviction in November 1975 for underground activities detrimental to the security of the state of South Africa. In fact I was digging holes for the white rulers. The subsequent prison years constituted a laboratory experience of the mechanics of freedom.

Then, early in December 1982, came release — and captivity. Not only because I had become conditioned to tail-wagging, not simply because the mind was now sly like a hunted beast, but because I was henceforth to be made a convict of respectability and accountability. I have seen. I am responsible. I must report. And so I became hemmed in by my own books, by all these images which like spectres took possession of my eyes to deform my vision. And to top it off I am now asked to write introductions to my poetry!

We should be entitled — Fincheye said, quoting Tagore — to the right to freedom, the right to nature, the right to remember. I add: the right to the fuckup as creative principle. How could there be insight without a break in vision? The pressure to conform, from friend and from foe, is enormous and permanent; we all live and participate in the conspiracy of mediocrity; we are all sucked into the need to make believe that life is worth living — in particular each one of our individual miserable exist-ences. One has to fight for the freedom to be a failure, a heretic.

The debate would, however, benefit from being centred rather on the intimate interaction between freedom and effectiveness in the field of keeping the options open. It is not necessarily shameful to be living at the table of the political lord or that of the patron of the arts, be it as fool or entertainer. The wine is often good there. Nor is it intrinsically wrong to be a kept woman or a gigolo. But one should do so as the chameleon; one must not be a master of disguises only, patiently stalking the fly and rotating the eyes in different directions simultaneously, but willing, furthermore, to act as the transformer of situations and relationships. In Africa the chameleon (or 'walk-softly') is the agent of transformation, the bearer of tidings that there will always be life, from one digestion to the next, and thus immortality — but it must be noted that he can also be used as the main ingredient of a very potent poison. And remember the words of Ka'afir, the poet: 'At birth the chameleon is transparent.'

True, you will be defined in your continuing attempts to define the inchoate. I think Baudelaire called it 'correspondences'.

Clarity/Consciousness. By now it should be abundantly clear that I am digging for ways to continue undermining the perimeters, the boundaries of clarity, the 'established law and order'. More than death I fear the living mummification of understanding and meek acceptance; the arbi-trariness, the petrifaction resulting from felicitous expression and lucid definition. When somebody says to you: 'I know': put a stone under his tongue and slit his throat and read the red stone for meaning. When the weak-hipped intellectual advances whisky in hand to claim: 'We are the avant-garde': offer him/her a wheelchair and a *Playboy* to masturbate over.

Si Dios vive, todo está permitido. But the quest for freedom, acting as if you were free, imposes upon you the bind of having to make decisions *all* the time, from nought to nuclear. It is very tiring, alienating. (What is *is*; what was *was*.) The civic poet owes it to the community to be a thorn in the flesh, but also owes it to his fellow travellers to keep on tripping himself up – for the sake of his integrity which is not an attribute but a method, a tool for scraping the crap from his perceptions.

Consciousness is a matter of leaps and bounds and crack-ups and painful reappraisals. And then the slow knitting of the flesh. It is the flame licking and spitting at the wick of the spine. It is the flowing stream with 'sense' the occasional surface-flash that makes you think it may be stilled into a mirror. Consciousness makes no sense except that it may lose a syllable or two to become conscience.

I remember getting up at night in my cell, which was like a hole, to do *zazen* facing the dark concrete mirror of the wall. And a moon of nothingness would rise. I also remember Moucho Marx saying: 'I started from nothing to end with nothing, but all by myself.'

One thing is not more beautiful or more useful or more spiritual than the other. There can be no hierarchy of aesthetics. For me the practice of beauty shapes the private parts of ethics. ('History protrudes and it is concave.') Neither can there be a withdrawal from political or ethical commitment; there is no irreconcilable contradiction between the two, rather they are as two tensions of the same striving. Aesthetics flow into ethics which leads to action. An act of beauty is a political statement.

Responsible/Subversive. For there remains the anger at what we are doing to ourselves, the hunger for silence, the rage to create, the need to transform (and be transformed). No guilt. (*That* we have as legacy from the Old Man in the soil, and only in action can it be dissolved. In any event, we need it like we need a hole in the head.)

I believe we are much more alert to our surroundings than we can afford to admit. I also believe that we transmit far more sensitivity than we wish to know – by allusion, the non-verbal meanings of our rhythms and our sounds, especially by our hesitations and our stumbling, the structural gaps and omittances in our language. By the unsaid, in a manner of speaking. Which is another illustration of how the Law is a husk: made up of the *meaning* – worse, the *interpretation* – of words.

Part of the civic poet's responsibility is to recognize the interstices, to be the thin wedge that could split the cracks, to seize the distaff elements and the moments of disequilibrium. He must be able to exploit the dynamic dialectical relationship of illusion, or appearance, with reality – knowing intimately the myriad ways in which the one becomes the other. The poet must be subversive. By word and by deed and by word-deed he continues to detonate the responsible certainties – in an ongoing attempt to break into the apparent/void.

Frantz Fanon cried out: 'Oh, my body, make of me a man who will always be asking questions.' He also said: 'I don't want to chant the past at the expense of now and of my future. I only insist on one thing: that the enslavement of man by man, that is of me by another, should cease forever. May I be allowed to discover and to want man wherever he may be found.' And: 'The colonized "thing" becomes human through the very process by which he frees himself.'

The foregoing is concretized in a critical relationship to the Left – where to be of the Left means to subscribe to and to participate in the struggle for generosity and tolerance and international solidarity with those deprived of their freedom and their human rights; when it means the willingness to keep working for greater democracy and better justice and more power to the people; where freedom is defined as a continuous battle, and one is made to think oneself into being and to comprehend the origins and the mechanisms of social organisms; where elitism is refused and the bringing about of some new orthodoxy, some school of cultural terrorism and atrophy, another power monopoly – be it hypocritically claimed in the name of the tongueless proletariat – are rejected for ever.

And then to translate all the above into a praxis.

To Be/Or Not To Be. Is indeed not the question. Even in your 'no longer being' you should be a disruptive force. Death is an exile, a perch from which to jump further. You could die ridiculously, beaten to death in some sad wasteland between Rome and Ostia, or by slicing your innards open on a clean mat. Or you could continue living, feeding your slow suicide on metaphor and colour . . . I slip from dream to waking and back

133

again, from homage to derision, from emptiness to love. Books to write and pictures to paint and political consciousness to be broken open. To be an eye to the landscape, and be part of it? To be. Not to be. And to be.

Breytenbach
Gerona, July 1986
(*to the memory of P.P. Pasolini*)